SMOKE
Cigars And Men That Enjoy Them

SMOKE
Cigars And Men That Enjoy Them

FIRST EDITION

A Boner Book by
The Nazca Plains Corporation
Las Vegas, Nevada
2006

ISBN:1-887895-26-4

Published by,

The Nazca Plains Corporation ®
4640 Paradise Rd, Suite 141
Las Vegas NV 89109-8000

PUBLISHER'S NOTE
Smoke - Cigars and Men That Enjoy Them is a work of fiction
created wholly by the author's imagination. All characters are
fictional and any resemblance to any persons living or
deceased is purely by accident. No portion of this book reflects
any real person or events.

Editor, Blake Stephens
Cover Art and Photo by Corwin
Art Direction, Robert Steele

Dedication

The habit of giving only enhances the
desire to give.
Walt Whitman, 1819 -1892

Table of Contents

SMOKE
Cigars And Men That Enjoy Them

FIRST EDITION

Short Stories by
Andrew McDiarmid
© Copyright 2006

Rain

There are moments in time that people will remember for the rest of their lives. Moments that are fleeting, and other times when the moment lasted years, months and days. It is when we reflect back on them later....that life halts. When we wake up in the middle of the night after dreaming that a loved one long gone is alive, or that road not taken led to adventures we can only dream of. You then turn over see that the alarm clock reads 1:30 am. So not only were you jipped by a dream that was going wonderfully, but you have only been asleep for an hour. It was just a reaction to that double of bowl of triple chocolate ice cream with a tad too much fudge bits just before bed.

But for Simon, you couldn't watch a good "chick" flick without chocolate. It just wasn't right to watch "Joy Luck Club" alone, on a Tuesday night...without the comfort of Chocolate Ice Cream with brownie and fudge bits, drowned in toffee bits chocolate topping. It was the least the girls in the film would do.....right?

He rose from the bed and quietly shuffled to the bathroom, letting out an audible groan as he pissed into the bathtub instead of the toilet. It was bigger and would get a good washing down in his shower the next morning.

The thunder and lightning outside didn't help much either. In Texas you get two types of rain. The lazy rain that fell like water filled petals from a rose barely making a sound as they fall, or gutter washers....where nothing that isn't under a roof is soon under inches of rainwater with no where to go. May brought the latter to Houston with a vengeance. He had sat in his 24th story office...watching the storm whirl around his office all day. It was like watching the inside of a washing machine...on an 8-hour wash cycle. No soap, no softener at all...just scrip, scrape and nosh at Simon's office window.

He took the light rail to the HCC stop after work and had braced as he stepped out of the train. The rain hit him and immediately drenched his jacket and hat. This was the type of storm that people who drove a car would wave from their warm interiors at him. Almost like saying, "Hello poorfucker without a car, enjoying this summer weather."

In retrospect, he only had one thing to say..."Fuck 'em."

He flipped on the bathroom light and rubbed the several days' growth on his chin, and grimaced. He hated to shave. But not shaving meant no promotion at work. They liked em clean at his architectural firm. And if that meant finally getting to do more than print clean up and actually build his own designs for clients......then shave he would.

He clicked off the bathroom light and slowly made to the living room. Tapped the buttons on the stereo and soon instruments filled his living room. Glenn Miller filled the room with the sweet serenade of STRING OF PEARLS....and he danced around the room as the lightning outside flashed through his windows.

"Bah bah bah bah buppa da, bah bah bah bah buppa da" "123, 123, 123, 123, spin, turn, 123, 123, 123, 123" A gay man dancing with himself in the middle of the living room...naked....forgetting that his curtains are open to the alley. The flash of light and thunder seemed to encourage the dance. "Bah bah bah bah, buppa da."

Then out of his corner he saw him in the alley. Simon froze.

The man stood at least 6 ft 4 if not 6 ft 5. He wore a long dark brown raincoat. It covered him up completely. A cowboy hat, rimmed quite thoroughly hid his eyes, and but certainly didn't prevent the beard that protruded from the chin to hang against the jacket. The beard was at least 4 inches in length of dark gray hair.

It would take another flash of lightning....for Simon to move. When the light lit up a pipe stem held in the man's teeth and a smile as well, Simon rushed for the curtains and quickly closed them.

"Oh fuck..."

Simon listened to his heartbeat inside him louder than the music on the stereo.

"Why don't we just go outside and give him a show....Sy..." Simon said softly.

He peeked out of the corner of the curtain and the man still stood there. The rain had lessened some, but there was a steady trickle of rain...from the bill of his hat, dripping onto the coat and making its way to the dirt/mud road the man stood in.

Simon was both repulsed and turned on a bit. This was a goodlooking man. But it was 1 am...and it was the alley behind his apartment. It was just strange. He was startled even more, as he looked back from the clock to the alley...and the man had advanced towards his apartment building....towards him.

The smoke from the pipe was even more apparent as he moved to just below Simon's window but keeping within view. The smile under the hat...still grinning ear to ear had the naked man above him....entranced.

Simon froze and just watched the man. The bowl of his pipe brightening as he took a long puff, and the smoke was released through the beard following the beads of water down the jacket. This was just too hot to stop looking.Simon tried to smile back him...knowing that the man...couldn't see him looking out. Could he? He had moved far enough back. He felt his cock harden.

The man then motioned at his feet. Simon gasped as he realized the man was pointing at his feet. It was a motion telling him...to leave his apartment and come to that man's feet.

A non-verbal..."kneel before me."

Simon swallowed hard.

The motion repeated...with a release of smoke. A snapped finger then joined the gloved hand pointing to the bottom of the trench coat.

"Don't make me ask again...." That said.

Simon reached for his jeans shorts and walked to the door. The alley was behind him now. He couldn't see the man from there. He would probably be gone when he got to the bottom of the stairs.

He came around the bottom of the stairs to the gate...and the man still stood there in the rain. Not under the carport away from the rain. He certainly wasn't a homeless man. The man could be a psycho...maybe.

Not a homeless man.

Another puff of pipe smoke.

Simon froze.

Another puff of pipe smoke, and the repeat of the hand movement.

"Kneel boy" the hand said to him within his mind.

Simon stepped through the gate and came to the edge of the dry carport. The older man never moved. Never reacted to his approach cept to snap his glove and point at the ground before him again.

Simon looked around briefly.....as the rain really started to pour again.

He moved forward. The man in the coat smiled as he approached. Then he heard the man's voice.

"Take the shorts off boy. You wont be needing them anymore," Simon resisted.

"Don't make me ask twice slave...take off the shorts."

Simon did as the man requested.

"On your knees like a good boy."

Simon did as the man requested.

He looked down to be greeted by a pair of motorcycle harness boots. The type that had the buckle slide over the smooth leather of the boot and acted like a body harness for the ankle. His cock was hard again.

"Look up at your MASTER boy," the voice commanded.

He looked up at the coated man...and the smoke and smile seemed so much farther away from his vantage point. This close to the man the scents of the cigar and leather jacket were like natural poppers.

"I am Magnus, and you are mine now boy. I like what I see, and I always get what I want..." he said.

He then reached to the jacket's button and started unbuttoning them. From the middle…..he reached inside….and pulled out a very large uncut cock through the holes. The foreskin hid a full erect cock.

"Take my flesh inside yours…and it will be your last decision till my training of my slave is over. DO YOU UNDERSTAND ME SLAVEBOY?" the voice questioned.

This was a moment….Simon would always remember. That question asked of him. Before the changes began, before Simon became Sy for good…..and Master Maximillian's prize slave boy.

"Yes SIR I understand."

The smile on the coated man widened…as the jacket released the rest of the way up. It revealed a muscular body with several tattoos that glistened with sweat from under the jacket. There was gray and black fur everywhere. The pipe smoke was sliding down the Master's fur, leading his eyes to the pipemaster's cock.

"Come to me slave," the voice commanded.

Simon moved forward on his knees and took the man's cock into his mouth. The precum was sweet and a welcome taste. Two leather-gloved hands wrapped around his head and pressed the flesh of his Master's cock deeper.

"Good boy, you are all mine now."

The lightning flashed. The thunder roared. The rain encompassed them and sleep was the last thing on Simon's mind.

CAMP

Part One

It is the red flower that greets him in the morning. It is in the moments of the dew from a new day that he found most of his peace. When the others traveling with him haven't wakened yet, to disturb the natural balance with their campy banter. When boom boxes playing music for breakfast, and the sizzling of bacon and eggs indicated the beginning of another day of camping. Walking through the towering bushes of red flowers, all that Charles needs in the early morning light is the rhododendron fields, and the colors they reveal. He cherished his friends very much, but just walking among the foggy hills through the natural garden was going to be a highlight of the trip.

Charles Foster lived in Portland, Oregon and loved it there. The city provided enough of the big city lifestyle that he cherished, but provided a wide array of other arenas of pleasure as well. The spring and summer brought the camping season, and his friends would go on a campout a month. The wonderment was something he really appreciated in this stage in his life.

He could remember being led to the same places that the camping brigade led him. His parents trying to show him every corner of the world as a child, was something he took with him into adulthood. Even at the age of 39, he still found nature was the best campground. Oregon Dunes National Recreation Area was one of the areas he remembered most. Not just for the red and white flowers that were greeting him, but for the towers of sand that the forest would soon reveal. North Dunes was his favorite trail, and as the dark greens trees gave way to the mountains of sand, part of him was home.

He could remember flying along the paths with his brother, on bicycles. The laughter and the warmth that it brought him were irreplaceable. Nature always brought the best out in people. It was in these settings, that his family seemed to work. Sadly, it was in the city that the same family seemed to drift apart. His brother rarely spoke to him since he was "out". Gregory Foster didn't need anyone to know he had a gay brother. It had been that way for 10 years now.

As the dunes began to surround his vision, he took solace in the quiet morning. For once the sun rose completely, and burned off the fog the sand would be covered in tourists. That had traveled here for the Florence Rhododendron Festival. He enjoyed the excitement of the festival as well. His friends of many years, made this annual trek with the knowledge that it was a weekend of bonding and getting away from the city.

He took a stride off the path and climbed one of the main dunes. He reached the top of the dune to find it up within the fog. He was glad he was wearing a jacket as the fog wrapped around him. The cold of the fog quickly immersed him in another world, and he just kept stepping. He knew this dune well. Soon the climb ended, and he found himself at the peak. He sat down on the sand, and removed the thermos of coffee from the backpack.

The warmth felt good against his hands.

The liquid poured with great amounts of steam into the cup.

"And good morning." Charles said to himself.

He lifted the coffee to his lips and took a long sip. There was nothing else that satisfied this much in the morning. Well, there might be one or two things that met the same satisfaction as coffee, but neither sex, nor a long hot shower were available.

He then heard footsteps coming towards him. That unmistakable trudge through sand sound got louder and louder as he continued to sip his coffee. Out of the dark mist appeared a tall husky man. He had a very large black moustache that dropped over his lips, and he wore a simple hooded style sweatshirt, with the hood up and adding to the foggy setting was the smoke from a large cigar. The ember lit up his face as he walked up to the summit where Charles was sitting.

"Ah, someone has discovered my secret morning place...." The man said.

His voice was deep and warm. There was an instant smile upon the man's face, to relieve Charles's nervousness on his approach.

"We must have missed each other before.... I come here all the time," Charles Answered.

"And with coffee...at that..." the man answered.

The man came up beside him and smiled.

"Well you mind some company?" the man asked.

"It's a free dune..."

The smoke of the cigar was very woody and aromatic. Charles was internally aroused by the source of the smoke. Both the cigar and the person smoking it were affecting Charles nicely. The cigar man removed his hood to reveal a nice flattop of dark black hair.

"Daniel's my name," he said cheerfully as he sat down next to Charles.

Charles fumbled at a response for a moment.

"I'm Charles...."

The two men shook hands. Charles offered the cigarman coffee.

"Never touch the stuff, much prefer a good smoke in the morning...." Daniel said with a wide-toothed smile.

"To each his own," Charles answered as he sipped more coffee.

"Can't ask for a better morning then this can you?"

As if by cue, the fog began to burn off from the top of the dune. It revealed the dimly lit forest and the other mountains of sand. The two men sat quiet for a moment.

The smoke from the cigar wafted cross his face.

"I'm sorry, i'm not meaning to blow smoke in your face..."

Part of Charles wanted to tell him it was just fine. Part of him wanted to say.... you could produce a lot more. But in the middle of a state park, in a conservative area of the world, was not one of those places.

"What brings you out here?" Daniel asked.

Charles proceeded to tell him of the friends he camps with. That most of them partied quite hard, and normally turned into "wild bears" if disturbed before 9 am. Being an accountant, Charles woke up at 5:30 am every morning whether he wanted to or not. Up and dressed by 7 am, it seemed a nice way to start the day to take his hike.

Daniel said he was with a group of campers as well. They were not far from one another in the campground. Charles had wondered if the cigar man was from the other slightly noisy campsite the night before. He didn't ask.

Daniel took a look at his watch and sighed.

"Well, damn it, if I haven't found myself with a handsome cub in the middle of the dunes, with a lit cigar…and I have to go make breakfast."

Charles took a deep swallow.

"Don't worry, I know you were at the other gay campsite…. helps when you see the gay flag, and the leather pride flag on your jeep at the grocery store…" Daniel said with a sheepish grin.

Daniel stood up. He reached down his hand to Charles, and offered to walk him back to the campsites. Charles took his hand, and felt the firm grip of the older man helping him up.

"Nice to meet you Charles…. you seem like a good boy."

Charles didn't know how to respond at first.

"Thank you, SIR."

He saw a glint of recognition in the cigar man's eyes. They began the descent back into the fog and to the trail below. Just as they reached the trail, and found the privacy of fog Daniel turned to Charles and released a large puff of smoke into his face. Charles inhaled almost hungrily.

"What ya know…a handsome cigar boy in the middle of the Dunes?" Daniel said with a large grin.

SMOKE

The two men walked back into camp, to find most of the people at Charles's camp awake and assembling breakfast. When they saw him with the cigar man, the voices all lit up.

"Well, now we see what Charlie has been up to...."

Charles thanked Daniel for walking him back and walked into the camp. "This is Daniel.... he is camped just down the way..."

The eight men in the campsite all waved in unison..."Hello Daniel"...

Daniel quickly whispered, "#5" in Charles's ear and continued walking.

"Cigar Daddies in the wilderness...you slut," chimed one of the campers.

Daniel continued walking towards his campsite hearing the loud cheer of congratulations behind him. He couldn't deny the hardon that the boy had given him. He was thankful that the baggy sweats he was wearing didn't give the boys back at Charles's campsite....a more revealing show.

Daniel stepped into his campsite, and found his tent still neatly closed. Beside it was a Winnebago. Two men in robes and a naked man cooking breakfast greeted him upon entrance.

"Good morning Gentlemen...."

"You and your hikes..."

"Found a camp full of girlfriends down in number 8"

The two men at the table laughed.

"Anything promising..." Asked one of them.

"Actually there is a very handsome cigar boy among them..."

"Tell us more..."

"Not much to tell, although he had a wonderful first response to my smoke"

"Well, maybe this weekend will be a fruitful one after all, Daniel."

The other man then stepped up from the table and walked to the naked man cooking breakfast. He opened his robe to reveal a half hard cock.

"Time for your morning feeding...pup."

The naked man knelt and took the robed mans cock in his mouth. The morning piss flowed into the man's throat and was swallowed hungrily.

The robed man tapped the boy's head and smiled.

"Good boy...now go make sure, Uncle Daniel and Daddy are taken care of..."

A simple, "yes SIR" came from the kneeling boy's lips. He crawled across the carpeted floor to the other robed figure.

"May I have your piss SIR?" the boy asked.

The second robed man said yes, with a gentle smile. He parted his legs and the sound of swallowing again filled the air.

"He is getting much better at this ..." the second robed man said.

"Uncle may I have your piss?" a quite voice the requested.

"Fetch boy..." Daniel said sternly.

He felt the hands of the boy pulling the sweatpants down. He felt the warmth of the boy's mouth around his cock. He felt the kneading of the head of his cock. The boy wasn't cock sucking; he was in search of piss.

It soon paid off.

"He is such a piss pig..." Daniel said with a chuckle.

As his piss poured down the boy's throat, he wondered if the boy at campsite #8 would do the same for him. He wondered many things about that handsome cub. His cock hardened cutting off the last bit of piss.... from the piss drinker's throat.

"Back to breakfast," the first robed one commanded.

The boy popped back from under the table and returned to the kitchen.

"There's plenty of time for sucking Uncle's cock later...." Daniel reached under the table and slid his hard cock back under his sweats, letting the precum make a visible wet spot in the dark grey pants.

The Rhododendron Festival might not be a bad trip out of town after all.

Part Two

Charles walked into his campsite and listened to all his friends chuckle and laugh. For most of his 30's, the six men and one woman in his campsite had been his family. Two couples, and a rather loud straight woman who preferred the company of gay men, than other straight persons was his family. There were Freddy and Clark; Two men that were the epitome of what gay men called bears. Freddy was nicknamed the "walking carpet" which of course was one of the major reasons Clark adored him. The other couple was Clive and Daryl. There were two men that had refused to leave the 70s. Their tastes still lay in Donna Summer, relaxing tea blends, and a never-ending quest to convince Daniel at that only could TOFU taste delicious but ... it was good for you. So far they had not succeeded.

"So, only our little Charlie could find a cigar daddy all the way out here in the sticks." Freddy laughed.

Charles could only smile and nod his head with an agreeing smile.

"Actually he found me...." Charles answered.

That was when the woman of their group chimed in. Her name was Josephine Rodriguez. She insisted in everyone calling her "Josie","you know like Josie and the pussycats..." Well, except for the fact that this Josie...was 5 foot 9 and 400 pounds, there was little resemblance to her namesake, cept their need to accessorize in cheetah patterned clothing.

"Well, I am personally happy for Chuckles...he hasn't had a man in his life for a while, and hell, if that one has a brother...find out if he's straight!" she said.

"And on that note. Breakfast is now served...."

Charles turned towards the breakfast table with a note of caution.

"Who was in charge…. please tell me no healthy breakfast…?"

Freddy laughed.

"Don't worry, we'll leave soy burgers and brussel sprouts for the lunch crowd…." Clive slapped Freddy on the shoulder.

"Its alfalfa, and it'll burn fat …," he said as he rubbed Freddy's stomach.

The group of friends dove into a regular breakfast of cereal, bagels and sundry fruit they had found at the market the night before. They all ate hearty knowing that the dunes would produce a long day of fun along the lake. The group ate healthy and as they were cleaning up they saw the cigar man from earlier once again walk past their camp.

Josie immediately chimed out.

"Hey there Daddio, we'll see you on the dunes!"

Charles wanted to hide.

The cigar man waved at them all, and then made a second specific wave in Charles's direction. Charles shouted hello and waved back. The cigar man was soon joined by three other men…. Daniel was his name if Charles remembered correctly. While he was lost in thought, he didn't have time to stop Josie from running over to the group of men. He couldn't hear their conversation, as he continued to put breakfast up. He only got more worried as the loud giggle came from Josie, and then silence, followed by another loud giggle. She came back into camp.

"Fabulous, we'll see you there…." Josie came rushing back into camp to Charles with a large smile. "They are joining us for lunch…."

"I can see the headlines now… 'Butch men die of Tofu poisoning'," Said Charles.

Clive came out of his tent joining in the laughter. "If our burgers don't kill them, Josie's femineity will. I mean gawd its like having three women in one body."

The four men tried to make a quiet exit from the campground.

SMOKE

Daniel just wanted to get as far away from the large woman as possible. He personally saw coming to the country as an escape from giant fag hags. "Josie" as she called herself was the specific type of woman that made him glad he was gay. In fact, proud of the fact he was gay.

Daniel had found the boy's shyness appealing. It was nice to have a younger man interested in him, but not throwing himself in prostate at the first sign of a cigar. It was clear though, that the boy liked the cigar and its smoke. He would have to make sure that he was on the dune the next morning waiting for him. No rest for the wicked as they say. Regardless of whether the boy was trained or even interested in a leather type relationship Daniel was going to enjoy the banter till he found out.

Mark and Tony, and their boy Troy, were laughing and giggling after him.

"Well we have to all agree Josie is the perfect choice, but will she fit in your tent," Mark said.

"The two bears.... had more hair that Daniel has, I didn't think that was possible," Tony added.

"Please no Speedos, on any of them. Specially the woman."

Daniel gave them a simple but pleasant glare.

"You are just as twisted as she is, just in your own way," Daniel laughed.

"You are comparing us to her!" Pup retorted.

Daniel laughed at the boy.

"Most of all you, with your shrine to Christina Aguilera in your bed-room at home, and your incessant need to listen to music that was written by a computer instead of a piano," Daniel answered.

The boy pouted. One of his Daddies reached for the protruded lip, and it quickly vanished.

"Don't tease your Uncle like that, it might mean no more piss for you today..."

The boy seemed to auto-retreat into a silence. Daniel reached with his hand and rubbed the back of the boy's head.

"I don't know. Not feeding him piss, is a strong punishment..." Daniel said to Mark.

Mark rubbed his goatee in agreement. "We'll think of something, I do so enjoy tormenting my pup."

The four leathermen climbed into the dunes now covered with scattered enclaves and groups gathering for a day at the lake. They took over an area that would accommodate them, and the new found gents from the other campsite. As Daniel placed the last sheet down, the sled whooshed past him.

Ah yes.... it was going to be a good day. The sled was the beginning of the show. The lakeside of the dune dropped in a sharp angle, and the bottom of the dune, as well beneath the water line. People brought plastic sleds from wintertime and slid down the dunes, flying up a man made sand ramp, and flew into the water. Daniel pitched his umbrella, and laid down his cooler. It was nice to have a day that was just going to be watching other people enjoying the water and the sun. One or two water coolers and some suntan lotion, Daniel would lie out and enjoy the constant flow of the people he considered insane take their plunge down the hill.

He then saw the pair of leather sandals, and furry calves come into view. He looked up to see the cub from the other campsite standing in knee length boxer swim shorts, and a white t-shirt. It was a laundry detergent ad, cept instead of the brand; it said "QUEER" in bright while letters against the familiar rainbow of the detergent logo.

"Good morning once again, mind some company?"

Daniel swallowed softly. The man-boy-was very handsome.

"Sure...have a seat..."

The young man was very well mannered and was soon joined by his friends.

"You found a good spot, great for sled watching, you ever do it?" the boy asked.

Daniel laughed. "Ah. No. never been that dumb..."

"Well, Freddy and his partner have a larger sled built for two ... we will easily fit on it..."

Daniel started to resist the young man's charms, when the other two Daddies came up to them.

"If you convince Daniel here to fly down the dune, you'll be good in our book."

Daniel simply shook his head no.

He still didn't realize how many wine coolers, and prodding it took, but there they were in the sled. The older man shook with almost visible fear. Charles wrapped his arms around him and smiled.

"Don't worry. It's the water that will be cold, but its over quickly."

The cigar man turned to him and tried to force a smile. "You will owe me so bad...if I survive."

And with that Freddy came up behind them and gave a good push.

"Have a good trip you two..."

With that the sled plunged downward over the sand. It would be many years later, that Josie told the story of mothers reaching for their children's ears as the sled took off. Daniel proceeded to yell curse words all the way down. Some even she hadn't heard before. The only thing that stopped the string of obscenity was the splash of water.

The two men surfaced in the water, to the applause of the crowd.

Daniel's hair dropped down into his face, and Charles trying to prop him up. He was visibly shaking.

Daniel swept the hair back from his face turned to Charles and laughed.

"Oh yeah, we're doing that again..."

Daniel grabbed Charles arm and began the journey back to the top of the dune. They talked about life back in Portland, and were genuinely excited they both came from the City of Roses. Turned out they went to a lot of the same places.

The cursing filled the air again as the sled flew past and up the ramp.

As they came to the water's surface after the fourth trip down the dune, Daniel lifted Charles in a large hug. Daniel then quietly released Charles, when they both felt arousal in their swim shorts. Maybe in the front of a bunch of straight people at the beach wasn't the time for a dripping wet French kiss.

"You look like a drowned rat all wet." Charles laughed.

"Oh Really?" Daniel answered.

"Well, a handsome rat."

The two leathermen and their boy watched from their lunch spot with a smile. The boy named Charles was truly having a good time with their friend. It was a long time since they had seen Daniel truly have a smile on his face. It had been three years since his last partner had died due to complications of AIDS. Daniel was slowly coming out of his shell again.

"I like the boy…" Mark whispered in his partner's ear.

The cursing filled the air again as the sled flew past and up the ramp.

"I like him, a lot."

Part Three

It had been four days since they had returned from the dunes to the rainy skies of Portland. Charles sat at the table sipping on his tea latte and gaining depression from the fog and the rain. The dunes had been blessed with wonderful weather, and allowing the first enjoyment of the summer's coming sun. The city always seemed to hold on to spring longer than Charles appreciated.

He ran his finger over the cup of tea, and found himself always chuckling at the name. How a coffee shop in Portland would be called Seattle's Best Coffee, always made him laugh. They were just as numerous as Starbucks, yet another Seattle import. He had never been able to drink coffee, no matter how many times he tried. He was quite capable of making a good cappuccino when asked to, in fact he actually bought the machine, but drinking it was right up there with tofu; it wasn't an option.

The trip to the dunes was just supposed to be a good weekend away with friends and it had become something much more. Meeting Daniel was not something he had planned at all. The man was quite intriguing. Knowing that there was a handsome man of his caliber that was single, had given Charles hope. But, Daniel Tosier was much more than just a single man. He was a leather man. Through the weekend Charles had learned a lot about the man, but was given the distinct impression that he had only scratched the surface.

The day of sliding dunes and lying in the sun was expected. Spending a quiet afternoon falling into sleep, in an older man's arms in a hammock was not. Daniel had made it clear that he was not going to be sexual with him and Charles had found that admirable. It was refreshing to find a man that wasn't completely focused on sex and getting that good blowjob and forgetting to provide a phone number when it was done. He had wakened up lying against the now familiar grey sweatshirt top, and the soft rumbling of Daniel beside him. It was a wonderful way to spend an afternoon.

Daniel had gone for a walk with him, and told him that he was looking for a partner. But not just any partner. Daniel was what he considered an old guard leatherman. Daniel didn't want a boyfriend, and specifically didn't want a "boy". The cigar man had been much more specific in his needs and desires. Part of the conversation had bothered Charles, but a lot of it drew him to the man.

"I want a sub. Not a sub in bed, a sub period. I want a slaveboy."

Charles had not understood completely.

"I don't understand SIR."

"There are men that will allow their subs to misbehave. They find attraction in the need of the boy to play, misbehave, and overstep their boundaries. I don't find that attractive. My friend's boy is frequently pushy and more of a pushy bottom than a boy. I want a boy who knows his place is to please me, and I am willing to wait to find the right slaveboy. It is an important difference. If I wanted a "boy" …there are millions of them on the Internet, right there in Portland. But I want more than that…"

The words made Charles tremble inside. Was he capable of what Daniel searched for? There was enough in his words, to be willing to explore the possibilities. That was exactly after spending the afternoon in the hammock. Daniel had called it, the sleep test.

"You don't snore, or toss round. I don't have to tie you up for you to stay still. It's just a requirement. And... you kiss well."

Oh yes, they had kissed. The cigar man sure knew how to really kiss a man. Charles almost became weak in the knees when it happened. It wasn't a peck of a kiss; it was a deep tongue massage type kiss.

Now, Charles had returned to work and found himself watching the business world go by on Main Street as his latte warmed his hands. Upon the table was the number. He stared at the card wondering if he should call. It had been three days. If he called first, would it be seen as being pushy? That was exactly what Daniel had said he didn't want. The boy wondered if he was out of his league pursuing someone like Daniel. Just as he pondered his future with the cigar man from the dunes, his cell phone beeped.

Someone had just sent him a message.

He lifted the receiver and as the message started…. he immediately recognized the voice. That alone was making him melt inside, warming him faster than the latte ever had.

"Good morning boy…you look handsome in blue. It flatters you…."

Oh God, Daniel was here.

"…I just got back to the office. I was touched that you sat there staring at my card with a dreamlike stare…"

"…. And I figure it is time for us to meet again."

Daniel sat in his office with a large smile on his face.

"We will be meeting this Saturday at the Chinese gardens. I trust you know where they are. If you don't…time to go on the Internet, and find …Portland Classic Chinese Garden. I am sure an intelligent boy like you knows how to find it.

But enough of the place. You need more information don't you boy.

There is a place in the garden that says "Double Happiness" in a place called "A Thousand Ravines Engulfed in Thick Clouds." You should be at this location no later than 1200 hours on Saturday. Don't be late. Being early is better than ever being late. It is Mr. Daniel's Rule #1. I know you'll remember that one boy..Don't disappoint me. Do not call me back. Just be there…"

Daniel hung up the phone. His cock was hard…. his Prince Albert flapping with the emotion that was filling him. This boy had potential. He'd need training. But what boy doesn't need training?

He turned back to his computer monitor and typed the simple sentence. "The invitation has been sent." Seconds later a single buzz filled the air.

"Now lets see if the boy lives up to his expectations," Daniel smiled.

"I believe he will…the waiting is going to drive both of us nuts."

Buzz.

"But you like it this way Daniel."

Daniel didn't respond with words, he sent a large smiling face, showing all of its teeth.

Yes. He liked this boy a lot. This was his form of foreplay. The boy was going to earn every drop of cum and piss.

"Get back to work," the screen buzzed.

"Having a loft....and working at home has its advantages."

Buzz.

"I hate you sometimes...."

Daniel logged off the chat program, and flipped over to the web page. The picture of the Chinese house intrigued him. It was always one of his favorite places to meet and talk with a boy. Too many wanted to meet in bars that led almost immediately to touching and fondling. Daniel didn't want that yet. He wanted inside Charles's head.

"Painted Boat in Misty Rain" was the name of the houseboat in the gardens was the perfect choice. "DOUBLE HAPPINESS" described the relationship between a MASTER and his slaveboy quite nicely. Both received happiness, but in different ways. One was incomplete with the other.

Saturday couldn't get here soon enough.

Part Four

Charles really didn't concentrate at work on Friday. Thankfully the Friday wasn't at the end of the month where he needed to work harder, it was mid-month, and his workload was light. He had a very quiet morning, and once all the supervisors left for the day, as they did by 2pm, he turned on his chat service and looked to see who was online. Freddy was there.

"Good afternoon Freddy."

"How is your afternoon of number crunching?"

"You know I wouldn't be on here if I was busy."

"The good thing, my dear Charlie, is that we talk amongst ourselves over here...so I have chat open all day."

"Yes, I know...rub it in, but then again because you chat all day is why I make several more dollars an hour than you..."

"And the gloves are off...."

Charles always loved talking with Freddy. They had known each other for so long that he didn't know what his life would be without the bear as a friend. Ever since Charles first appeared in the Dirty Duck and Freddy flew over to him wearing a pig nose. Charles had found himself moving into the city on the same weekend as the bear weekend. In the bear group, Freddy was the greeter. And of course that meant short shorts, no shirt, boots and a pig snout. Clark would then introduce himself, "I see you have met my little piggy." They were a monogamous bear couple. Clark sometimes seemed to be "forcing the issue" with some men. If Clark saw a threat in a new face, he immediately indicated they were married. It would take him several weeks of interacting with Charles to get over the protection, and allow the new man in town to become a friend. That had been 8 years ago.

"I have to go get a dew..." Charles typed.

"Blech."

Charles laughed, turned his monitor off and headed to the break room. He returned with two cans of the green soda and filled his sipper bottle.

He turned back on his monitor to find a new box on his screen. The chat service was showing that someone wanted to talk with him...who wasn't on his buddy list. He read the name, and a shiver washed over his body.

"DANIELSIR53" wishes to chat with you....allow? Oh god.

Below the request was a simple message.

"Good Afternoon handsome boy......I seem to have found you chatting at work."

Charles quickly screwed the lid on his sipper bottle and took several large mouthfuls of soda before responding.

"Good Afternoon SIR. I tend to be a good multi-tasker," Charles typed.

He then saw Freddy chime in."Back yet...?" He didn't answer.

DANIELSIR53 responded. "That might come in handy. Do you know who this is?"

Charles smiled. "One hopes this is the Daniel that I met at the Dunes...."

A small happy face appeared on his screen clapping his hands.

"Good boy"....

"Thank you SIR. Before we continue, the boy needs to inform you that they monitor my pc, and this chat cannot be explicit in nature..."

"Understood. Then don't open your email till you get home."

Just as those words appeared on his screen, so did the little white envelope in the bottom of his screen, indicating he had received an email. Then a small window appeared that read "Email New: Master Daniel's

Instructions for Meeting". Charles took several more gulps of dew.

"Received. Will review when I get home SIR."

"Good boy...I am signing off for now boy.... Say hello to Freddy for me. And thank him."

Charles grimaced. A conspiracy. "Understood SIR."

The DANIELSIR53 box vanished.

He reopened Freddy's box.

"You've been bad..." Charles typed.

A smiley face appeared several times, that seemed to be laughing out of control.

"He asked nicely...he did." Freddy responded.

"Your attempts at talking like Eliza Dolittle won't save you...He sent me an email."

"Open it ....!!!! TELL ME TELL ME"

"He said it wasn't a "work appropriate"...email."

"Now I really want to know what's in it!!!!"

"Patience oh furry one...on other news how is Clark?"

"He's packing for the trip.... I always let him pack. He is a genius."

"Oh that's right, you are heading for Chicago?"

"Yes for the bear Run, and darn IML is there too...wish you were coming..."

Charles smiled. "I have a feeling my Memorial Day weekend will be enjoyable in many of the ways yours will be, but with just one man involved instead of hundreds..."

"LOL!" Freddy responded.

"Back to work for me, something you'd know nothing about."

"Bitch..."

"It was said with love."

Charles stared at the little white envelope. It amazed him that a simple email could affect him like it was. His underwear would be covered in precum by the time he got home. He looked up at the clock, and it read 2:35 pm. Damn. Three hours.

Daniel once again had a large grin on his face. He normally didn't go to these lengths to toy and play with a boy before they met and went on what he considered a first date. He had hopes that this boy wouldn't be coming looking for an evening of sucking cock and nipple play. The email he had just sent was a short but simple change of plans. They would have a date in the gardens but he didn't feel that it was right for a first afternoon together so Daniel decided to change the plan of affairs. He would find himself in the gardens with the boy, if things went well. The gardens were a great place to discuss philosophy and the aspects of SM that scared most boys off. He needed to get a better take on where this boy could be led before getting intense. There was this part of him, that Daniel knew would respond to intensely very well. It was a place Daniel found himself a lot of the time. It was also why there wasn't a slaveboy at his feet currently. Daniel wanted the right slaveboy, not one who was there because there should be one.

He turned off the pc and turned to the CD player in the console behind him. He turned the CD and turned on track 10 of the current CD. A single oboe played the overture he was all to well familiar with.

The symphonic sounds filled the room and the voice began to sing. He stood up and began to sing along with the words.

He walked into another room as the music swelled. The violins filling the room with the type of musical orgasm that they alone were capable.

He closed his eyes and dove into the music.

The swell of volume begins.

The Chimes, and French Horns are added. The gentle placing of voices singing the tones swell underneath leading the soloist.

Then the one piece of truth. The one that holds true to many that are hurt in love. Daniel opens his eyes to the rainy day outside his window as the last words are released.

"People who hurt tend to put up shields; Protecting themselves ……………….my heart."

That last word held for over 30 seconds. And the cd fell to silence. It would be one of the first lessons for this handsome boy. Getting to his heart would be a task. Some would almost say formidable. But in Charles's favor…. Daniel Tosier hadn't chased a boy like this in many years.

It was 4 pm.

Part Five

Good Afternoon boy: Please don't think I was spying on you earlier at the coffee shop. I came in the side entrance, and got my afternoon latte, and you were ahead of me in line. You had your nose deep in a book, something about the Civil War I think. You didn't notice me, and that is also ok. I am not expecting you to walk through life waiting or searching for me. That would be unfair to both of us.

I know…. get to the point of the email. Patience young man. Patience. I will admit you have certain abilities and taught protocols that arouse me. But we both know that protocol can only impress so far. But I am not an easy man to impress, neither should I be. I believe I am a good Daddy/Master/ Dominant, so I firmly believe if I take a slaveboy on, he has to be of the same caliber. I can see you nodding your head in agreement, like a good boy does.

We are not going to meet at the gardens, although I can assure you in the future, we will meet there. You might even be taken there under duress or enforcement. Good, gets your mind thinking on those terms doesn't it.

We are meeting in Washington Park on Saturday at Noon. Bring a raincoat; regardless if it is raining…you'll need it. Don't plan on being home very early Saturday night, although you will sleep in your bed.

This game we call interaction is not one I take lightly. I have decided you are worth getting to know better. That does not necessarily mean, fuck you, rape you (although the thought of raping you. forcing myself upon you, is a grandiose vision, it is so much sweeter when you are restrained, and taken. With the knowledge that I am taking what is already mine.)

Please bring three CDs of your choosing, and have a good reason for bringing each. Don't test me on this, you are selecting music for not just me, but for you as well. Have a reason for each selection. I want to sense your passions. Your needs. Your desires. Your life. To see if your yin, takes a hold to my yang.

It is really that simple. To a point. I am not the perfect specimen. Neither are you. You are a tad overweight. You already admitted that to me at the Dunes. There are ways to help you with that. With and without my assistance.

Be at the Washington Park Max station, Noon. Be early, rather than late.

Early arouses me. On time makes me proud. Late makes me less interested.

Daniel Tosier.

Ps. For now…call me SIR. Only exception is when introducing me when we meet someone you know. I know you are capable of this.

Charles read the email again when he arrived home Saturday evening. It brought a great smile to his face. He hoped he had kept to the requests made in the email. The day had taken them far from Portland and had included a intensely deep meaningful kiss, cigar smoke, long conversations, and getting to know SIR. Daniel was becoming more than just a passing interest. Charles didn't know how to deal with a lot of the emotions that he was causing within his body. Most of all, it was the new elements that many had forgotten in the world of leathermen. They were dating. That did not mean Daniel was his MASTER by any stretch. That was one thing that Daniel made clear. It had begun by riding the rail that made one short stop to Washington Park, and hoping he was there early. The email had said, "Early arouses me". It was something Charles wanted to be accomplishing as often as possible.

The day was grey, and overcast, instead of the bright sunshine that the weather on Friday night had indicated. Charles stepped off his train into the station at 11:45 pm. He scanned the people waiting on the station, and he didn't see Daniel. He sat down on the bench and waited. The minutes seemed to drip by. As if he was in the slow motion section of a movie, where time slowed to a crawl. 15 minutes slowly crept by.

SMOKE

As Noon appeared on the clock on his cell phone, it rang.

"Hello, this is Charles."

"Good boy. You're there…"

Charles swallowed. "Good Afternoon SIR. Wasn't aware you had my number…. we were meeting at Washington Park SIR?"

"Yes, and if you look towards the art work on the corner, the wood structure…"

Charles looked over and saw two men he knew too well.

"You should see Clive and Freddy. They gave me your cell number, and let me know you arrived safely. They are good friends, aren't they boy?"

"Right now, I am only thinking evil thoughts towards them."

Charles waved at his friends, and they waved back enthusiastically.

"They called me to let me know you arrived safely. And they were pleased to tell me you were 15 minutes early. Such a good boy."

Charles laughed.

"You find my words funny boy?"

"No SIR. Just finding myself set up that's all."

"Don't worry boy. You are in good hands."

"Now you should see a blue train going east, get on it."

Charles stepped onto the train.

"Good Boy, now wave to your friends again, like a good boy should."

Clive started waving with both hands. Freddy gave Charles a salute.

"Now its just you and me for a ride across town. Are you familiar with the 102nd street station…"

"Yes SIR."

"Excellent."

The two men spoke about their week. The good points and the bad points, as downtown, the Willamette river, and the convention center slowly moved by. While Charles still found himself in slow motion, the voice over of Daniel Tosier was soothing and guiding. Daniel allowed him to laugh, and interact. Few men Charles interacted with before did that. They seemed so hung up on being the dominant, that life in general was lost as the result.

Charles began to feel Daniel was one of those men who didn't let any part of life slip by, and that life was to be celebrated. There was energy about the man that Charles couldn't quite put his finger to.

"You'll loose me for a while on your cell phone, call me back after you leave the Gateway station, where the redline moves north, understood. Freddy was kind enough to put my number in your phone during your night out last night..."

Charles laughed. "I so feel set up."

"Don't worry. Call me back."

The train slipped Lloyd Center. And soon past Gateway. He scrolled through the phone numbers on his cell, and came up an entry called "SIR."

He pressed dial. "Good Boy." the voice answered.

"Yes SIR."

"Did you bring the raincoat?" Daniel asked.

"Yes SIR."

"Excellent, you are going to be needing it. Now, a few couple of items before you arrive...are you opposed to cigar smoke?"

"No SIR."

"Excellent, as I don't plan on putting my cigar out for you anyhow."

Charles didn't respond.

"Secondly, when was the last time you came?"

"In the shower this morning…"

"Prolific with our jacking are we?" Daniel asked.

"I normally shoot 4-6 times a day."

There was a short pause on the line.

"So noted, slave."

Charles felt the tone in Daniel's voice.

"Remember, always end your sentences with SIR…no matter how distracted you get. Its good practice."

"Yes SIR."

The staircases leading up to 82nd Avenue appeared out the window.

He was close.

"Good slave…I know you'll work hard at that. I like that."

"Thank you SIR."

"Now, know you are mine for the day. And most of the night. Freddy and Charles know you are with me, and they are confidant, I'll bring you back in one piece."

"Yes SIR."

The train had paused just outside the station. As he watched the red line peel to the north, he began to breath harder. He was getting off at the next station.

"Now don't get antsy boy. Its just one station."

"Yes SIR."

The train continued on its path and Daniel asked if he was hungry.

"I had a bagel SIR."

"Then you are, but you can wait a while."

The train announced the 102nd street station. Charles stood up.

"I'm waiting on the platform boy. Hang up the phone."

Charles replied "Yes SIR" and flipped the phone closed.

As the train moved towards the station, Daniel was hard to miss. He stood at the end of the station, with a large cigar in his mouth. A full-length leather stormer coat blanketed his body. The train, and Charles passed him as a large puff of smoke left his lips. Charles smiled.

He stepped off the train and stepped up to Daniel.

"Good Afternoon SIR."

"Afternoon, slave."

Daniel pulled Charles into his arms and hugged the boy. They both felt some nervousness fade as they touched. Charles seemed to melt in the embrace.

"Come. Lots to do," Daniel said softly into his ear.

"Yes SIR."

Charles and Daniel left the platform and into their day.

Part Six

Daniel smiled as the music started to play. The boy had a very inter-esting choice. Daniel had always thought he was musical knowledgeable, especially of the 1980s. But, he had never heard this piece of music before. The boy looked on nervously through the thin veil of cigar smoke at him.

"So who is this by again?" Daniel asked with a smile.

"'Travellers' SIR."

There was nervousness in his voice still. Daniel knew he had to get the boy to relax. Maybe find someplace to pull off and get something to eat. Where they could talk in public and the boy could relax. Then Daniel real-ized that he wasn't taking a novice into the woods. This was a good boy.

He turned to the young man and smiled. He let a single string of cigar smoke fall from his mouth and down across his chest.

"Well, we can't be this tense the whole trip. It would defeat the whole point, wouldn't it boy?"

The boy smiled. It couldn't be that easy.

"So why did the slaveboy bring this CD of all of his?"

Daniel could see the constructed thought forming.

"Don't talk to me like an email boy. Open up and relax. You are with a SIR who likes honest interaction. That is a two way street."

The nervousness again seemed to slack in the boy.

"Travellers was my favorite band in the Navy. They just had words that seemed to speak to me. I actually brought this to talk about SM cause I figured we would be talking about what the boy likes, what YOU like, and such SIR..."

That's it boy...keep going...Daniel was encouraged.

"We close our eyes talks about resisting what is deep down inside of us. The thought within us that we resist our entire lives, till time is running out and we haven't lived as we could. Being a leather man I feel that emotion everyday. Cause I don't fit a mold. "The mold" SIR."

Charles flicked his fingers in the area forming the quotes. Daniel smiled.

"THE MOLD?" Daniel asked.

"Well it always seems that tops on-line in the community are always looking for the in shape, furless, young thing in his 20s, the muscle god. They want the exact thing that meets the ultimate fantasy."

"Maybe you have looked in the wrong places?"

"It is more than that. I am 6 ft 1 and 238 pounds. I'm not thin. I never will be. Just not built that way. I am turning into my father. Its like the tummy is hereditary."

The Master chuckled. The slave had potential for many reasons. The main attraction, well after the handsome face, was his intellect. This was a slave who truly felt who he was. He wasn't just reading out of the latest issue of Instigator or MACH21.

"Most don't like a furry submissive bear. I guess that is what I am. A furry submissive bear. But I was born for more than to just be a submissive. I like to serve, and finding someone who wants a furry bear to serve is harder than I realized." Charles continued.

"Well maybe the hours you spent on the Internet every week could be found better spent elsewhere? How long have you been uncollared?"

Daniel said with a half smile.

The boy stared out the window to his right, and watched the river drift along the right side of the freeway.

"Too long...SIR."

Daniel liked the emotion of the slave as well. The slave wasn't just a cookie cutter there were emotions that would need to be focused.

"Don't be coy, slaveboy...talk to me" Daniel said as he laid his gloved hands on the boy's leg. His leg physically shivered.

"7 years. And actually I thought I had gotten used to the fact I was alone. I used many things to mask the needs that are inside. SIR."

Daniel was getting the boy to relax and tell his story now.

"But then why are you in my truck going somewhere you are not aware of?"

"Because I have the feeling you are capable of understanding my need to serve...and can focus it. Whether for you, or someone else. I just get a good vibe from you SIR.."

Daniel saw the Willamette River come into view. It would be soon be time to get off the freeway. He saw the boy trying to make his bearings.

"Ah, I know where we are now....SIR," Charles said.

"Don't get down here often boy?" Daniel asked.

"Well when you don't have a car, sometimes the suburbs are something you only read in the paper...SIR"

"Well there are many things down here you haven't experienced yet..."

Daniel smiled. Charles did as well, in a shy way. Not all the walls had come down for the boy yet. There would be time when all his walls would not interfere, but erased by a Master. Maybe this one. Daniel didn't know yet. There would be no walls for him to hide behind by the time he was done. He knew that. If the slaveboy continued to please him, the thoughts and accomplishments with this young man would be endless.

"So you don't find yourself on the Cascade Highway often?"

Daniel pointed to the freeway overpass talking about the upcoming exit.

Charles laughed, "Not lately SIR."

Daniel found himself thirsty.

"Could you use something cool to drink boy?"

"Yes SIR."

"Well let's get off here at the McDonald's and get two cokes through the drive through. We have about an hour drive ahead of us. No stopping.

So get something to eat if you wish to." Daniel said.

"I wouldn't mind getting something, not a meal, just something to keep me better to later…"

"Good boy. Keep me informed of your needs. You might not always get what you want but…. we'll work from there."

Daniel pulled off at the next exit and made their way to the McDonalds. As they pulled up to the drive thru he asked Charles what he drank.

"Root beer. No caffeine."

Daniel smiled. You learned something new everyday.

"Two Root beers, and a mighty kids meal with nuggets"

Daniel turned to the boy and saw a smile on his face.

"Three nuggets each. Keep that in mind. I tend to be territorial about things that are mine…" Daniels said with a grin.

That brought a huge grin to the boy's face. Daniel reached over and ran his hand over the boy's head.

"Root beer and Nuggets it is."

Daniel then tried to remember the exact directions to where he was taking the boy. He leaned over with the cigar in his mouth and released smoke right in the boy's face. There wasn't the expected cough, instead there was a distinct inhale from the boy. He liked smoke. Good to know for later.

Daniel took out the pocket map of Oregon out of the glove box and dropped it into the boy's lap. The plastic fell very nicely between his legs.

Daniel reached over to get the map from the floor of the cab. The cigar came close the boy's crotch. He quickly sat up.

"Your mission if you choose to accept it."

The boy froze.

"Say, Yes SIR, I accept the mission," Daniel said in a slightly sarcastic tone.

"Yes SIR."

The drive thru attendant suddenly materialized.

"Thank you."

Daniel dropped the two sodas in the holders between him and the young man. Dropping the bag of fries and nuggets to the armrests, Daniel turned to the boy as he placed the cigar in his ashtray.

"Well let's have a rest here by the river, before heading into the hills."

Charles agreed.

"Now. Your mission should you accept it, is to keep tabs on the map. We are in fact going south on the Cascade Hwy. Hwy 213. Let me know when we get to Silverton. That is our first stop. Understood boy?"

Charles smiled.

"Yes SIR."

He picked up the nugget and tried to eat it like it was something he did regularly. He noticed the boy didn't touch the fries. They hadn't been talked about yet. He quickly ate his three nuggets and left it at that. Daniel turned to him with a quizzical look.

"Hmmmm. I wonder."

Daniel took the still lit cigar and took a deep drag on it. He then grabbed the boy's head and forced his mouth open with his own. He released the smoke and he could feel the moan within the boy form and release.

"Yes…. you do like smoke…"

With that Daniel, put the truck in gear and asked the boy.

"Ok, where to……………"

It was 1 pm.

Part Seven

Charles found himself singing along with the CD as the mountain air filled the cab. The fine wisp of Daniel's cigar was teasing at him from the ashtray and was a wonderful reminder of the breath of smoke.

He had been a little shy and taken aback by the man's actions. No one had ever just reached over and forced smoke into his mouth and lungs before. Well, there had been fantasies in the darkness of his bedroom stroking his cock to the rhythm of the ceiling fan above. But it had never happened.

"Lets get an understanding right away....my handsome young pup. I wouldn't have you in my cab, if I didn't want you here. I wouldn't feed you my smoke like that if I didn't have a sexual attraction to you, and find your current physique attractive. We both agree you could loose some weight, and you shall. But you wouldn't have made it even this far, if I didn't find the current package attractive."

Charles smiled.

"Good. Now...where to boy?"

They found themselves flying down the Cascade Hwy away from Interstate 5 and all the hustle and bustle of the freeway. Small little farms and homes went by, and the short 40 miles from Oregon City to Silverton, were second CD that Charles had selected to bring along. It was AIDA. Charles noticed the wince in the cigar man's facewhen he mentioned Opera.

"Its quite a romantic tale....I like the quiet parts..."

"I don't know the story.."

"Well, it is about a MASTER finding there is more to a slave than just work in the palace. He finds a bond with a female, who also happens to be the princess of the people Egypt is currently enslaving. It talks about the struggles of wanting of a love forbidden but so desired..."

Daniel seemed to be receptive.

"But not in an SM sense, a real slave," Daniel asked.

"Yes SIR, in a slavery type way. But they fall in love regardless."

Daniel smiled. "Proceed."

The music filled the cabin of the vehicle, and the woman spoke of the wonder of tales of love. Her quiet gentle voice filled the cabin behind the rich tones behind her. Charles smiled and turned to Daniel waiting for that moment. When quiet becomes rage. It was a deceptive introduction. The softness of a flute, keyboards, and her gentle tones; only to reveal that slavery isn't something soft and gentle. Egypt was a power to kneel too. The music exploded in sound and volume. Anger piano, and guitars blossomed.

Charles went to turn it down. Daniel met his hand with his own.

"No...let me hear it boy..."

Daniel took the boy's hand into his and clasped it as the music continued.

The princess's introduction letting go into the introduction of the Male MASTER; talking about the power of Egypt.

The Master's voice filled the cab with words of pride. Charles yells over the music that this is the lead actor. Daniel smiles. He listens to the music the boy brought, and finds himself awed that even the male's singing has moments of sweet softness. The first song ends, and the cab goes silent for a moment.

"Very interesting pup."

"Glad you approve SIR."

"AIDA," the pup introduced.

Daniel smiles inside. He then is surprised as the pup's voice enters the cab and sings with the woman in her range. This slaveboy had passion.

It was one of the things that first attracted him to the younger man. Few men of his generation showed this side of themselves. It was nice to see the barriers finally slowly lowering and the slave was letting Daniel see all of him. Not just the cute, attractive parts. The two voices held the long note at the end of the track.....and Daniel smiled.

"You sing well..." The Master said to the slaveboy sitting beside him.

Charles grinned ear to ear. "Thank you SIR."

Charles told the continuing story of AIDA and her future love. Daniel listened contently as he saw the mileage between Portland and Silverton slowly lower. It would be in Silverton where the real journey would begin.

For in Silverton they had erected a great set of murals. The history of Oregon put upon great canvasses. If there was a boy he could have brought here, it was quickly becoming apparent this was the right one. There were eight in all. He had to make sure he showed the boy the murals in the right order. Because their final destination was on one of the murals.

"May I speed up to a track to play for you before we get into town SIR?"

Daniel winked at the boy. "But that would ruin the ending."

"Promise it won't SIR."

Daniel squeezed his hand. "Show me pup."

The young man turned to him with serious look and said, "this is when the slave realizes to save her people, she has to tell the MASTER she's not in love with him." Daniel began to see the passion in his eyes as he spoke.

Charles sang with her and his hand tightened around Daniel's hand as he sang. He could see the boy's chest fill with air, and then burst out as he carefully kept up with the soloist on the CD. Some would just be impressed with the boy's lungpower. There was a lot of sound coming from him even for a bear. The slave smiled as he sang the words occasionally looking at Daniel possibly seeking for a response. Daniel hid his words; he wanted to hear the whole piece. He felt the warmth in the boy's touch. He felt his fingers slowly rub against, his hand.

Silence.

The boy reached over and turned the CD off just about the time the welcome sign for Silverton appeared.

"Well I believe I'll take control of our voyage for a while young man," Daniel said as he released the slave's hand.

"Yes SIR."

Daniel shut the CD off as the small town began to greet them. He searched for the right turn. He also hoped he had memorized the map correctly before leaving. They came upon the first mural, and he smiled. Good. They were on the right side of the murals.

"These are the Silverton Murals."

"Oh yes, I saw these in the paper when they erected them SIR."

"Excellent."

Daniel parked the truck alongside the mural and motioned for the slave to get out. They walked up to the white wall, and the four-panel mural of people greeted them. One was of three generations peering off into the sunset, each having their own dreams. Secondly, they found a young man that seemed to speaking at a town hall meeting. As they shuffled down the street they found the third panel of the traditional thanksgiving feast, and then a fourth panel, of a father and his son.

"They are very classic in presentation, like that guy who drew those drawings in the 50s..." Charles said with a smile.

"Norman Rockwell....SIR?"

Daniel looked at the panels and agreed.

"Hmmm. You know you are right.... looks like a little project for the boy. Find out about these drawings. Maybe it is Norman Rockwell....well back into the truck, one more to see at the edge of town."

The Master didn't know if he could keep the secret from the boy for much longer. He was never good at hiding good things, or bad things for that matter.

They made their way through town and they shared the other murals; Some showing the last 100 years, some showing the pioneer spirit of the west, and some just showing the history of the town around them. Daniel knew there was only one left. He sighed as it began to come into sight. It read SILVERTON, then in smaller writing "the falls". Within a circle on the mural, was a single waterfall.

"Silver Falls....I haven't been there since childhood..." Charles said.

That did it.

"Well good, because some friends of mine, and your friends are waiting for us at the campground. But we have one more walk before we join them..."

"Where SIR?"

"The Trail of Ten Falls boy. And you get a treat at each one..."

"A treat SIR?"

Daniel grinned under his stache.

"The slaveboy will get to taste a part of me...at each waterfall. Or at least near each one."

Charles swallowed deeply.

"The 10th fall, you'll get a very interesting taste boy."

Daniel smiled as the road started to climb out of Silverton and along silver creek. He reached over and retook the boy's hand.

Charles looked as if he would never stop grinning.

It was 4 pm.

Part Eight

Daniel had noticed as they left Silverton, that the boy had brought two other CDs. It had a bright red tribal pattern on it, with no words. He smiled and put the third disc in. Violins and loud tap dancing filled the cab. The cigar man turned to the boy in question. The boy smiled….as the violins were replaced with electronic music.

The electronic sounds filled the cab as the woods surrounded the view of the road ahead.

Charles paused the CD and the silence was a striking change.

"It is the theme of a spy film, it's actually the soundtrack…."

"And why does the boy like this cd in particular. What makes it different?"

Charles smiled at the cigar man. "Well, for several reasons. The lyrics, are talking basically about the mentality that one might have while being interrogated. Through the opening credits, flashing of the spy being tortured are played…various types of torture…." The boy paused…biting his bottom lip…" and will admit to liking the singer and this being a more adventurous piece for her."

He then began to wonder how much thought the boy had put into the choosing of the three CDs he was instructed to bring with him. Wondering was the boy's home clean, and structured….with all his CD's neatly in a row, or just in a large cardboard box, unorganized and taken by random.

There was so much to learn about this slaveboy. He already saw much potential, but didn't want to put the horse before the cart, quite yet.

"Also the whole soundtrack is the bond theme mixed into dance tracks, and upbeat rhythms. The whole soundtrack was out of the norm...for a bond film. It showed that the spy had a weakness, and that sometimes he gets caught. It shows the spy as a more human character..."

Daniel reached back and turned the CD back on, as they climbed into the mountains.

Daniel hearing the last part of the boy's comments, he sped the CD forward to start listening to the instrumental soundtrack. While slightly ironic to have the theme filling his ears, but at the same time finding solace in it; the boy had been right....this wasn't his father's spy soundtrack, leave alone his.

"It is also a great CD for mummification, you can loose yourself in the music. And the beat...and go off to that world that mummification can provide" Charles said.

That took Daniel by surprise. The boy was finally relaxing and talking SM with him. That was a good sign. So was the rising hardness in the boy's jeans. Once again, he could see the boy standing in front of a mirror, deciding on whether to wear the tight jeans he has chosen, or going with baggier clothes. He actually enjoyed the thought of the boy trying to figure out which would most please him. The more Daniel talked and interacted with this boy, he knew that...part of the boy's attraction was his innate effort to please. It wasn't an act....it was just who the young man was.

"May I play you my favorite track before we get to the top SIR?" Charles asked softly.

"Of course, boy."

Charles smiled and flicked the CD forward.

"This is called A Touch of Frost."

The soft and repetitive beat of the Madonna song filled the cab, but at a muted restrained level. Then a piano breaks into sound, and the beat dissolves into a march like ballad. It is softer than the rest of the music they had heard thus far. Just as one got used to the softness of the piano, the beat returned....and dance a quick, and symphonic taunt. The track ended.

"Its short, but really effective."

Daniel smiled inside. The boy was unaware of what awaited him at the top of the grade. He just continued to share....talking softly. There was a gentleness to the boy that the cigar man found intoxicating. But he also knew that as the soundtrack.....there was a wild aggressive side to him. He looked forward to tapping that energy and making his flesh ripple.

The short 15 miles of driving from Silverton to the edge of the park soon came to an end as they entered the park. He slowed to the lower speed limit and found the North Falls Group Camp area. He slowed down and pulled into North Falls parking lot.

"Time to grab your raincoat boy......time for a walk."

"Yes SIR."

Charles grabbed his coat and opened the truck door, and found the coolness of the mountains greet him. He knew they really weren't that high in the mountains, but the suddenly rise in height from the valley floor at Silverton, left a crispness in the air. The parking lot was full of the normal large amount of cars and the area was buzzing with activity. The boy stepped out and put his raincoat on. He stared through the cab at the cigar-man that had brought him to the falls. His mind raced with all the possibili-ties. The dark haired man had him in some stage of arousal since he had met him at the rail station. The smoke feeding back at the river was a high-light. He had been dreaming of that moment since he saw the first cigar the man lit around the campfire back at the dunes.

At some point he would tell this man how much he had enjoyed sit-ting around the fire with that man's arms around him, slowly making their way to his nipples through the flannel shirt he was wearing. Randomly tweaking them, letting the boy know the Daddy wrapped around him was more than just interested in him. It left him with a hardon that he couldn't release.

His thoughts were broken by the close of the truck doors and the squack of the alarm system. He jumped in surprise much to the amusement of Daniel. He could see the soft but subtle smile forming. God, to kiss this man. He hoped that would be on the agenda for the day. Do Masters kiss slaveboys...he hoped to find out.

"Just the alarm boy.....thought I had you relaxed..."

"You do SIR, just lost in thought..."

"Well then we have a walk ahead of us don't we..."

"Lead on SIR."

Charles smiled brightly. "With pleasure boy..."

Daniel came around the truck towards him, with the raincoat flowing with his body. He reached into his jacket. And pulled out a cell phone, handing it to the boy.

"Press 6, tell who answers the truck is ready for pick up."

Charles gulped audibly. He looked down at the phone and a cell # had been entered but not completed.

"Press 6, and send. Boy. Don't make me wait."

"Yes SIR."

Charles for a moment connected with Daniel's eyes. He obeyed instantly.

The phone had begun ringing when he put it to his ear.

"Yes SIR," a voice answered.

"I have been instructed to let you know the truck is ready for pick up..."

"At North Falls lot?"

"Yes SIR."

There was an audible almost high pitched giggle on the other end of the phone.

"Thank you."

Whoever was on the other end hung up.

"That was strange. ...," Charles said.

Daniel raised an eyebrow.

"How so slave?"

"Well, the person answered, and when I called him SIR, he almost seemed to giggle."

"Samuel must have answered the phone.....you'll meet him later. Isn't the most butch boy in the world, but his daddies love him."

Charles went to comment, but the Master continued talking.

"Well, the truck is taken care of...now its just you and me for two hours boy...here is my watch. Please notify me of each half hour."

4:30 pm.

"Well our little adventure begins there..." Daniel pointed towards the east. "We start at upper falls...but first make sure you get the pack out the truckbed. There are two full waterbottles, and one empty one. Bring all three."

Charles simply went and got what he was told. A school size back-pack laid in the truck bed, clipped to the webbing that covered the truck bed. He unclipped it and turned to find Daniel right up against him.

He could feel his pulse quicken as the man was closer.

"I'm glad you are here boy," Daniel said.

He reached over and ran his hand over the boy's head, and Charles craved the touch. There were so many other places his hands would be welcome.

"Thank you SIR."

Daniel grinned and again pointed east.

"To Upper North Falls, where our journey begins."

The two leathermen walked across the highway and up the well-maintained trail. There were a lot of people heading west down the other embankment.

"Didn't know there were falls this way," Charles said.

"Well, the more spectacular falls are that way, the ones with all the ooohs and ahhhs. And we will go down into the canyon, it is on the list. I plan on shoving my tongue down your throat behind North Falls..." The man paused. Both for effect, and to smile, "...patience is a virtue my young man."

He had said "my" ...and Charles beemed. It was a tad premature to be thinking of totally surrendering to this man, or was it. Were there steps he had to take...?

"Snap back out of thought boy...."

Daniel rubbed the back of his hand again. It almost seemed like a mental tether to the boy. He shivered at the touch. The type of shiver that reached down to the base of his ballsack and stayed there...vibrating.

"Sorry....just enjoying looking at you SIR."

"I'm not that special..."

"To me you are....SIR."

"I know boy. I wouldn't have brought you here if I didn't feel you wanted to be."

They could hear rushing water.

"The falls are in full bloom today. June is a good time to come see them. The water is crisp and cold...and makes for a great mist," Daniel began.

"First of all these falls up here, as you see, aren't visited by nearly as many people, and are just as beautiful."

They came down a clearing to the river bed and across the avenue of rushing water, fell Upper North Falls. What struck Charles first is the difference in the other falls from the park, and these falls. Their descent to the river bed below was a much shorter distance. It was if God took the tall slender falls, that were numerous in the Oregon Cascades and squished them. They were a wide niagara type drop. They were wide and majestic, and as forecast by the man he was with....the mist was everywhere. The water cascaded over the top of the falls and hit large rocks at their base. There were a few people at the side of the river watching the falls, and there was a bridge that crossed just below of the falls. Daniel motioned Charles to cross the bridge.

"We are going up the canyon side....a short distance" the man said.

Charles followed the man.

They started up the canyon into the lush greenery. Daniel turned as the falls came into view through the trees. He turned to the boy and smiled.

"Now...we are alone ... good. Hand me the empty bottle."

Charles complied.

Daniel then reached down and unbuckled the stormcoat from the bottom up...quickly revealing that above the boots, there were no trousers. Soon the unbuttoning revealing a semi hard....uncut....large...fat...cock.

Daniel didn't bat an eye.

"The empty bottle slave..."

Charles fumbled it forward.

"I have had a piss hard on since the murals..." Daniel said softly.

Charles was speechless. He couldn't look away from the cock as it slid into the now open bottle.

"Like what you see boy?" the cigarman asked.

"Oh god yes...SIR," the slave answered.

Piss started flowing over the pierced pisshole of the MASTER into the bottle.

"After proper training, we wont need a bottle. But you will drink my piss like a good boy. Won't you?"

Charles tried not too seem to eager.

"Yes SIR...I will."

"Good boy..."

Daniel shook his Prince Albert to ensure every drop landed in the bottle. He removed his cock and let it fall against his leg. He reached to the piss lit and found a drop of piss on his finger. He raised it up and said "Taste me boy."

Charles opened his mouth gladly. The bitter taste of the piss was gently put upon his tongue. He clamped down on the finger and it made Daniel growl.

"Taste, not suck boy."

Daniel removed his finger.

"Time check."

4:50 pm.

"God. Plenty of time for sucking later boy. And trust...me ...you will."

Part Nine

He still could taste the lingering of piss on his tongue when they passed by the bridge and upper north falls. It wasn't a strong piss, and he'd been noticing that Daniel had been drinking mostly water, cept for the root-beer back in the valley. What struck Charles even more, was the smile on Daniel's face; as they walked and talked it didn't seem to fade. The smile widened every time Charles took a swallow from the sipper bottle. It was like they were walking along the path, interacting with each other, nodding to people as they passed, saying "afternoon.." all the while Charles drank the entire bottles worth of Daniel's piss. By the time they had reached the parking lot, the piss was gone. Conversation had turned to continuing down the hill. It has been many years since Charles had seen the actual North Falls. There was nothing like them that he knew of. The falls had a unique-ness all their own.

Charles looked over to where the pickup truck had been parked. It wasn't there.

"Ah…SIR!!!…the truck."

Daniel's smile returned anew.

"Let's just say that the truck has been taken care off….all your stuff in it is fine. We have about two hours of walking ahead of us, and we should be there by dark. But for now, nothing settles piss better than a nice cigar…"

"Taken care of SIR?"

"Just accept the fact, you are with me for the night….the truck will be back."

Charles smiled back at the cigarman as the flame leapt across the medium sized cigar. The embers lit up the end and the deep aroma filled the immediate air.

"Come boy…North falls awaits."

Charles knew right then, didn't know why, just knew right then he would be able to follow this man to places no one else had taken him. They walked through the rest of the parking lot and towards the falls. North falls was high enough you could hear it much sooner than you could see them. As they reached the top of the downgrade into the canyon, Daniel stopped and pointed at the sign.

"Ok young man, you've done a fine job of directions so far. Our second goal of the day is twin falls. Ready boy?" Daniel asked.

Daniel turned to see a slightly glazed look in Charles's eyes.

"Yes, SIR more than ready…."

Daniel reached up and rustled the boy's short hair. "Good boy, only 77 steps down to the bottom."

Charles followed the man but tried to stay within a safe distance to smell the smoke. Ever since the day on the dune, Charles knew he wanted more of it. Not just the occasional taste, but wanted to feed on it. They walked down the steps and through more people. The roaring of the water got louder.

When they reached the 77th step, the mist met their face.

"Well, boy I promised you tastes today didn't I?" Daniel asked.

"Yes SIR," Charles said with a suppressed excitement.

"Follow."

Daniel led him from the main path towards the falls. Charles followed the cigar man under the mist, as the path led behind the falling water. The crowd lowered as the mist increased. Now Charles knew why they were wearing raincoats. They stood behind the falls and looked out through the falling water. Daniel motioned for Charles to stand in front of him. Charles leaned against the rail.

"It is quite spectacular SIR."

Daniel then came in behind Charles and pressed his coat fully against the boy. He was sure that the hard cock that laid underneath was obvious to the boy. He felt the boy stiffen all over his body.

"The boy seems to be having a good effect on me, would you agree boy?" Daniel asked.

Charles felt the cock rubbing against his jeans. It was large.

"Yes SIR."

Daniel then whispered in his ear…"I hope you are enjoying this as much as I am…."

Charles shivered at the brush of goatee against his ear.

"Turn around."

The boy turned to watch the cigar man take a large inhale on the cigar. Daniel then grabbed the back of his head and forced smoke down his throat. Charles shook at the heated warmth pouring down his throat. Daniel quickly retreated.

"Hold it. Boy. "

A loving couple walked by. They stared at the raincoated men, and kept walking.

Charles was about to loose his breath.

Daniel then became serious again.

"Release slaveboy…."

Charles released the smoke from his lungs and mouth.

Just as he tried to gasp for breath, Daniel kissed him. The tobacco flavor filled both of their mouths. Charles shivered inside. Daniel pulled back and smiled.

"Like that taste boy?"

"Oh god yes…"

Daniel chuckled.

"That seems to be your new tagline."

Charles looked at his wrist.

"5:30 pm SIR."

Daniel laughed deeply. He took a drag on his cigar and smiled.

"So it is....time to head down the trail boy....twin falls awaits..."

For both men, there was more there waiting for them down the path.

Part Ten

There are times in your life where it can seem, an hour can be a week, or a month of time, can go by in seconds. It all comes down to whom you are with and what you are doing. If you wanted time to fly by, that is what normally occurred. If you took each minute of the time you had, and cherished it, the time would mean more after it is past. For Charles, spending time with Daniel meant just that. They walked along the river's shore and talked about life. Finally he seemed less nervous round the cigar man and he began to talk.

"I am not talking too much … SIR?" he asked.

"No boy…. I'm a good listener, and I happen to be liking what I am hearing…"

Charles had been asked to talk about what he wanted in a relationship. That was a hard topic to talk about, but he just took comfort in who he was with, and began to tell his version of a relationship.

"I want a one on one relationship. No more of this, I want to sleep with other people crap. Or….we are secure enough in our relationship to see other people."

Charles swallowed; expecting a response from the leatherman… what he got was…a puff of smoke.

"I need a man that understands…what commitment, romance, intimacy and kinky means, without it having to be brought up. I am just as comfortable naked lost in a man's arms in the twilight of the day, as I am in a full tuxedo, with a butt plug in my ass at a premiere of the latest touring play SIR."

Daniel had smiled at that last comment.

"But there are some things I want different, if I enter a relationship… this time…not necessarily with you…SIR."

Daniel stopped walking and turned towards him.

"No. Don't put what you think I want to hear in the answers, I need you to open to me as you, not as what you think I want to hear..."

Charles smiled. God this man affected him. It wasn't enough that the man looked ungodly hot in that coat, and that he was naked inside it. It was that there was intelligence pouring inside him. Churning, and staying inside and making him smile, unlike the constant stream of cigar smoke from his lips.

"Understood SIR..."

"Continue..."

The cigar man began walking again.

"I want to have a man who wants to fuck me. Not just 'fuck me' ... but has to fuck me. Just like I want to be addicted to drinking his sweat and cum, and the occasional gut full of piss...I want him addicted to the idea.... of fucking my ass. Needing my furry ass around his cock regularly....SIR."

Daniel chuckled.

"I also want a man that appreciates more than just a leather pair of chaps. To be able to walk through a library and talk about the latest books we are reading, he has to like movies, and not necessarily.... needs to go to the bar...regularly SIR."

Charles looked up at the woods.

"Being here is a good step forward..."

Charles motioned his hand towards the cigar man.

"No, this is not something about you particularly. We met on a dune on the middle coast of Oregon, not in a smoky bar. Don't get me wrong I love your cigar, but one is fine, 40 mixed with nasty cigarette smoke is completely another. I hate coming home from the bar...smelling like an ashtray...needing a shower to get the scent out of my skin....SIR."

Charles then briefly...took a gander at his watch. 6 pm. They had made it quite a ways down the canyon.

"It is 6 pm SIR..."

Daniel rubbed his hand on the back of his head.

"Good boy...we are right on schedule..."

Charles smiled at the cigar man.... just stopped and looked in his eyes.

"What is it boy...?"

"I like your eyes...SIR."

"You are off the subject...boy..."

Daniel was enjoying this walk with the boy. It was filled with little chances.... to taunt the boy with the pleasures of the flesh. Oh yes...they were there.... and before this weekend was out...the boy would get two.... really good tastes. But that was yet to be seen. The boy was finally opening up to him. He was having the rotating effect of getting his cock drippy, and pleasing his mind. The boy had his shit together. It was rare. It was too early to reveal to the boy that the soundtrack to WICKED and INTO THE WOODS, was in the center console. There are some things an inquisitive boy will just have to figure out on his own. There are times that boy's are trying so hard to be "just that"...that it was nice to find a man who was naturally submissive, and wasn't putting on an act to get laid.

Daniel had specifically picked this day to try and get the boy to open up to him. The phone calls they had during the two weeks between their meeting at the coast and now had felt scripted. If this was the boy that was going to be wearing a ball stretcher around his balls, and have his cigar lighter at pride in two weeks, he had to know him. Boys don't get Daddy's lighter by being a good fuck. There had to be more to a slaveboy that just a good piece of ass.

"Off topic...tsk tsk," Daniel said softly.

"So tell me...why a man who likes to fuck..?"

Charles shyed away.

"Don't clam up on me now...we have a climb ahead of us soon, and need to make sure you are worthy of taking all the sweat...from all of the places.." Daniel said firmly.

He waited to see how the boy would react.

"Most people enjoy my oral skills so much.....they forget about fuck-ing, or just plain aren't interested... SIR."

Daniel laughed inside and out.

"Ah. I've found a consummate cocksucker have I?"

Charles seemed to put up several layers of protection...visibly with that comment.

"Ok....wrong term maybe..." Daniel chuckled.

Daniel saw the discomfort he had caused. He had to fix it.

"Don't worry.....I am not a clod all the time boy...I was just kid-ding..."

Touch him on the back of the head again. He seemed to like that. The boy was almost trembling at his touch. When he moved his hand back, the boy moved his head to stay with it.

Daniel growled inside.

"It's been a longtime since someone found my sweet spot that quickly," the boy said softly.

Daniel's hand stopped moving away, and began to stroke gently against the bristly hair with his glove. The boy seemed to almost melt. Daniel was getting aroused again. They had to get up the canyon wall soon. Not just because daylight was running out....shoving this boy to his knees, pulling out the pa, and pounding his throat, and yelling "that's it slaveboy. Swallow your master's meat. The only meat you will ever need again..."....probably wouldn't go over when that family that was about 5 minutes behind him...caught up.

"Well, it seems we have come to our ...junction...up is our goal. Brisk pace, creates more sweat..."

The boy launched at the trail.

Teaching this one would be hard and easy at the same time. There was past training, and that was always harder to remove and replaced with the correct.... proper training. Also...he had an eagerness that made him want to fuck him. Fuck him into such a submission that he would never recover.... not that Daniel wanted him to recover.

The boy.... would do well. How well, yet to be determined.

It was 6:15 now...dinner was at 7 pm. God. That was going to have to be a quick throat test. No time to clean the boy out for plugs. But he'll get used...to a plug. He'll be getting used to a lot of things.

6:15 pm.

Part Eleven

The journey continued with the climb up from the riverbed. The climb was one of those times that always reminded the cigar man why he had to limit the number of cigars he smoked. He almost found himself out of breath several times, but he was damned if he was going to show that to the young man that he had been leading along all afternoon. There would be several tests in the evening ahead. Some intentional, and some.... misunderstanding, but that was what made life interesting. They still had so much to learn about each other.

"So show tunes aren't really your thing are they SIR?" the boy had asked.

Daniel had to laugh.

"What makes you ask that, boy?" the cigarman replied.

"Well, you didn't really seem that familiar with the cd's I brought with me..."

"I will admit to Andrew Lloyd Webber burnout...its all the same..."

"Well, there are other musicals..."

"Guess I assumed that one show was much like another...."

"You would be surprised what modern Broadway has to offer..."

Daniel loved the way the young man spoke. He was educated. Some many club boys, and dancing queens were still wondering how many different outfits Cher might wear in her next video, or who was seen where. This young man wasn't driven by gossip and trends. A nice rarity found.

"Well there is a musical about the wicked witch of the west."

"Don't we already have the wizard of oz?" Daniel asked.

"Well, yes, but what if it was the wizard that bad guy, and the witch just misunderstood…"

The kid had a point.

"So, there is more to life than just musicals however…"

"Sorry, SIR…. it's the effect that singing in a chorus has on me. It tends to make me want to search out vocal music. Not this Cindy Delane processed crap…"

Cindy who?

"I personally enjoy piano music. Almost my whole collection of albums. And yes, I still have some records, are Windham Hill. I find some of the work quite relaxing…"

Oh god, a bench. He needed to sit down.

The boy looked at him with whimsy.

"So does the boy get to find out what is at the top?"

The choice of words affected him.

"Third person, you have done that before…"

"Sorry, it's a habit. Many of the SIR's I speak to online like that type of speech…"

Daniel pondered how to respond.

"There will be times I prefer it from you boy…and time I won't…. just never met someone who falls in and out of that speech so fluently."

Charles thought he might run into the same bullshit he always ran into. It seemed a lot of men lived in a fantasy world where experienced boys were just not a wanted commodity. It was the moment that he revealed his experience to the cigar man that part of him gasped. Not wanting to hear the reaction.

"I studied for a year under a MASTER. We all spoke in third person. If we didn't, he didn't interact with us. It was part of the training..."

"Tell me about it...but we have to keep going.... dinner waits for no one...knowing our chef."

Charles took a deep breath and stood up, offering the older man a hand up.

"I found myself one of nine slaves, to one MASTER. We slept on mattresses around this huge bed. We were chained to it..."

He turned to look at Daniel, searching for a reaction. There wasn't a significant response to his words.

"Only those who didn't.... move in their sleep, or snore ever got to sleep in Master's bed. Alas, I was always on the floor...but as a unit we did everything together. Cook, clean, watch movies, goes to the bar, and of course, sm."

Charles smiled.

"But even the sm was a group activity. One didn't get paddled, everyone got paddled. One didn't get flogged, we all did. It was part of his training. We were supposed to reach down inside us and find ourselves..."

Daniel unintentionally laughed.

"What was your self, pup?"

"That was part of the problem, while I compartmentalized the pain and the flogger hitting my skin, and released a sexual arousal in the interaction, I never found myself barking, crowing, flying, seeing the experience through another's eyes.

He said lifting quotes in the air.

"There was one time that we were at a retreat, and a woman brought out a knife. We were put in a row, and we were asked. To give ourselves and our souls to the experience, to release our slave; I didn't really react the way the others did. Later, Master asked why.."

"Well, I knew who was holding the knife. To make fake peril, isn't true to oneself."

Master put me face down on a low-lying mattress on a frame. And flogged me.

He kept flogging me, even though I cried out and screamed.

He kept flogging me although I was releasing mucus in a puddle on the floor from my tears and screams.

He said I had found my self...

Daniel looked at the young learned man as they continued their climb.

"But you didn't?"

"No, that next day Master had us all up on the bed. He turned to me and requested...."how do you feel today slave?"

Charles laughed.

"You know there are times that you say the gayest things. Master wasn't really that gay focused. There was a real lack of sexual interaction not only amongst his slaves, but also between the slaves and their MAS-TER.

I thought to myself..."there was only one way to answer. "MAS-TER.... have you ever seen A CHORUS LINE?"

"No slave I haven't."

Several of the slaves nodded their head; and the senior slave smiled as if knowing what was coming.

"I am reaching down to the bottom of my soul.... and I am feeling nothing."

The slave that was slave Charles broke into tears and began to explain how it was not getting anything out of this interaction. That all the slave could feel during the flogging the previous day...was.... doesn't he realize I am screaming for it to stop. Doesn't he realize that all I am getting from this experience is the pain? I am not finding an anything.

It was that afternoon that my collar was removed by the MASTER and never placed around my neck again. Thought his tribe has grown and shrunk since...I learned the gift of submission from him. Just not the gift of finding something spiritual in the type of SM they practiced. Many have found great solace there.... but I swore at that time...I would find one man. And please him. Period. Not with others. One on one SIR."

Charles found himself in the embrace of the cigar man.

"Good boy..." Daniel whispered.

Then they kissed. Charles was stunned for a moment, and then found the warm tobacco flavored tongue of his new acquaintance invading his mouth. The feeling was wonderful.

The kiss released as suddenly as it began.

"We are going to get along just fine pup..."

Then Charles heard voices.

"I believe we aren't far from salvation..." Daniel said as he took the young man's hand.

Charles wrapped his fingers around the man's hand as he led him down the path. They came around the corner to find three trailers, and found tents. Around the campfire were Clive, Daryl, and Josie; with them were some new faces.

"Bout time..." Josie said in a loud voice.

A tall man came from one of the trailers, and immediately brimmed a wide smile.

"Good ...dinner's ready."

Charles suddenly had the feeling he was the only person not knowing what had been planned. Dinner was served at 7 pm sharp.

...Daniel laid in the silence of the long fallen night and felt the warmth of the man beside him.. There were so many memories from not just the day but from the evening. The jar candle was still flickering on the bedside table, and it allowed him a candlelit view of the young man beside him. To his word, Charles Foster didn't snore; he vibrated, almost like a cat that purred in his sleep. But then was a distinct vibration to his body.

He reached over to the candle and blew the flame out. The darkness that night provided quickly enveloped the couple, and the cinnamon scent of the candle began to be mixed by the wonderful scent of cooling wax. It hardened his cock against the other man in the bed. To any other observer that would be the extent of the scene, only two men knew that the submissive in the bed was also handcuffed, and was wearing a leather jock-strap. The dinner was a wonderful evening…. the memories of the evening began to flow as he fell into sleep.

Tomorrow, the training of his new slaveboy would begin.

TIME

The dark walls of the bar made Richard's skin tremble in anticipation. Living in a different part of the world, the leather bar in Chicago was
even more than he had anticipated. It was Memorial Weekend, 1989. All the
stories he had read, and all dirty magazines describing the experience of
walking through the bar had not prepared him.

The scent of leather and sweat filled the room. There were men of
every shape and size. But it was the man with the thick red beard who
intrigued him. Tall, muscular, tattooed, jeans ripped in all the right places,
nipples almost wanting to rip through the well worn t-shirt: All his research
had been correct.

The man let go of a puff of smoke from his cigar as Richard slipped
by him in the crowd and Richard felt the firm grip of a man's hand on his
ass. He turned, but couldn't see reaction from the red-bearded man,
because of the reflective sunglasses he was wearing.

It had been several hours since Richard had pissed, so he headed
to the bathroom. Again, it was the some old story;. a long trough along a
dark thin space. Richard slid to the end of the trough and took out his cock.
His bladder was full. As he began to release, the recent scent of smoke
filled the room. He turned towards the door and found it blocked by the red-
bearded man. The cigar flared in the dimness of the light in the trough area
as the man began to speak.

"Hey boy you keep pissing like a good boy I am going to join you."

Richard didn't know what to say. The large man came up beside
him and grabbed his ass again. This time Richard stiffened.

"You like piss boy?" the man asked.

Richard didn't know how to answer. He stumbled over an answer.

"I'll take that as a yes cocksucker."

A strong red-furred hand grabbed the back of Richard's head and he was forced to bend over. He soon came to face to face with a fat uncut cock, dripping with piss. He tried to back away from the cock, but couldn't get out from the man's grip. The uncut meat soon slammed up against his face. The bitter smell of man piss soon overtook him.

"Open that cock sucking mouth boy," the voice commanded.

Richard did as commanded as the tart liquid starting pouring into his mouth. He started to gag, then found if he swallowed regularly the gagging stopped. Soon the stream of piss lessened. The grip on the back of his head however didn't.

"You need my cock in you don't you boy, yeah you do, When I let my cock out of your mouth you better say. "Yes I want your cock MASTER."

Richard shivered inside as he pondered his new instruction. The grasp of the hand on the back of his head aroused him so. The scents of the dominant mans cock and the skin underneath the leather enticed him.

"Yes I want your cock MASTER," he said as he slipped the uncut cock out of his mouth.

"Good."

A cold metal slipped around his neck, which was something he was not used to. There was also the sound of a lock clicking closed.

"Get the fuck up asshole!"

The hand that had held his head so firmly in place dropped to his neck. The cold steel that had fallen round his neck tightened. Richard rose as the metal collar that now encased his neck. He found himself face to face with the powerful, red bearded, leather-clad, cigar smoking man.

"You are going to come in handy tonight boy as I am in really in the mood to break in a new piece of boy but I warn you my cock in your ass means you are mine fucker. And when I fuck a boy, and my cock plows his ass, that hole is mine till told otherwise."

Richard stood dumbfounded.

"You understand me boy?" the man asked.

SMOKE

"Yes, I do SIR."

The cigarman smiled.

"Almost thought you weren't going to say SIR, and we cant have that now can we?" he said as he released another puff of smoke.

Richard breathed in deeply.

"Come on boy, we need a taxi."

As they turned towards the door, Richard felt the room tremble. The cigar man seemed to have frozen in place. The ember on his cigar stopped flickering in the darkness. The scent of the new man that had placed the collar around his neck began to dissipate. Even the familiar scent of the piss trough vanished into a sense of cleanliness. All the sensations slowly faded away to be replaced by blinding light.

Richard stood in shock.

"Not now damn it, my hour is not up yet."

The dark piss hole of the leather bar had melted away. The dark black walls that had been the motif of the wall melted as if under great heat. Richard flinched as the bright light with which he was all to familiar with flashed through the room.

"God Damn it. My trip wasn't over yet!" Richard yelled.

"Your heart rate went way up, I was worried," the voice answered.

Richard Gentry found himself in the diamond transportation cage. He could still feel the chain around his neck; at least he hadn't lost that. It fell softly underneath his lab coat. His leather chaps, white T-shirt, and boots gone. Replaced with his lab coat, and form fitting lab shoes.

"Your heart rate went way up, what was happening?"

Slowly the light lowered to the point, that the laboratory that he had spent the last 10 years building and perfecting came into focus. In front of him was a short man in a similar lab coat.

"Your vitals went all over the place," The man said.

"Put it back on."

"You know I can't, once I reverse we have to wait 24 hours before maintaining the field again."

"You interrupted at a really bad time,"

The man behind the controls smiled as he saw the hard cock showing through the coat.

"Oh that is what was happening?"

Richard looked at his partner with anger.

"Yes damn it. That's what was happening."

Richard stood up and walked over to the mechanism. The diamond walls still had a specific date code and ethereal location identifier. He could go back, and the man in the leather with that ungodly handsome red beard would never know he left.

"What was it like?" the other coated man asked.

"Terry, the stories we have read about the late 1900's are all nothing like actually being there, you will see."

Richard smiled.

"So you are going to try to send both of us back to that point in time aren't you,"

Terry came to Richard's side and smiled.

"And how do you explain that?" he asked as he pointed to the collar around Richard's neck.

"I love the 20th century."

The Hunt

When you are as old as I,
Is anyone as old as I?
What difference does it make?
An offer comes, You take.......
John Karder
San Francisco, 2002

The ride on Bart was a slow one. But it always was when he was aroused and horny. Most nights that he rode the Bart home, it was to go home to his apartment, say hello to the building cat, flop on the couch and see what the local news had to offer. On the weekends there were other goals. Instead of taking the Bart to the suburbs, he was taking it back into the city for a trip to the local sex club.

But this wasn't like any other sex club; it was more like a bar with sex. If you went to a sauna, you would check your clothes in your room, walking around in a towel. For Marcus, this leveled the playfield just a little too much. It made everyone basically the same. It also brought in all the elements of the community. Nothing like cologne covered Twinkie walked up to him, and start gawking at his pierced nipples, and tattoos.

"Did it hurt?" ... "Oh Gawd, I just could do that. I just think your hot," all the while being nasally bathed in Polo for Men. Oh yes, that was quite arousing.

No a bathhouse wouldn't settle his hunger this evening. He would probably start at Daddy's in Castro, for a beer to settle his nerves. Many had always told him he needed to get over shyness, but a one beer or maybe two relaxed him enough that shyness wasn't the normal strong barri-er it was on most days.

He stepped on the Bart downtown, knowing he needed to transfer to the train above. The platform was quiet, just a couple of young lovers holding hands and waiting for the outbound train, and one or two singles. He walked to the escalator, to find himself reaching the moving stairs at the same time as another man. Quick review showed this wasn't just another "man." This was a god.

Marcus found himself looking up to a man about 6 ft 2, with a dark grey beard. Not a well-trimmed beard like most men, this was a thick bushy beard; the type of beard that hid the teeth even when someone smiled. He was also dressed in a well-kept storm trooper jacket. There were leather gloves on his hands, and two cigars poking out of the chest pocket of the jacket. Marcus visibly swallowed as he motioned for the man to go ahead of him.

"You first pup," the dark deep voice insisted and the leather gloved hand motioned towards the escalator.

Marcus stepped on the escalator and started the long ride up. Thoughts pouring through his mind; ok … who is this guy? Goddamn he is handsome. He smokes cigars as well…did I bring my lighter. Am I his type?

......

The pup was definitely dressed for a night out. He could tell that right from the start. No boy wore jeans that tight and tattered without wanting a firm grip put upon his ass cheeks. No one wore jeans that showed how much fur was under those jeans, with discrete but specific rips in the fabric. The first thing Maximillian noticed was how the boy smelled of sex.

This was a horny pup. His favorite kind….

Maximillian was hunting. The pup didn't know any better. But starting off the evening with handsome furry pup offering him the right of way, was just what he needed. The human probably wasn't aware of the fact that it was the full moon before Halloween, and it meant it was the beginning of his hunting season for a new human mate. This pup had …possibilities. Riding up the escalator with his tight furry ass in his face, only made the storm trooper jacket a better thing. It hid the enlarging hard on that was growing on the inside. Some lucky boy would get to lap up the precum this specific young man was producing.

But you never just pick the first hungry pup you find. There were mistakes in taking the first pup you find to your cock. You didn't find a quality servant by just taking the first that aroused. Most of the 1600s had been spent with a cocksucker who loathed the service, and did it solely because he had no choice. The scars on his flesh were also evidence of that same servant trying to kill him. Maximillian needed a servant that wanted to be there. At his feet, for 100 hundred years. He had not found one that warranted renewal. Humans, despite the gifts they received, rarely could devote themselves to him ... willingly for a second period of service. Humans almost always...wanted something new...something with a different taste.

Oh god, that butt. This boy would get fucked brutally by some man tonight. Any man who didn't take this boy into his den, and fuck that furry ass, and passed it up, was just another stupid human who didn't know what was in front of him.

When they reached the top of the escalator, the boy headed for the Metro station, towards Castro. How convenient they were going to the same place. More time to review the boy's actions....and desires. They slipped through the turnstiles, and the boy hurriedly went to the far left escalator...and walked down the moving steps. Maximillian let the other escalator casually bring him to the new platform. It never stopped to amaze him when you transferred at Market Street MUNI station from Bart; the whole world seemed to change. The amount of people on the platform tripled, and came from all works of life. He suddenly had many scents in his nostrils and the raging hardon under his coat receded. He reached into the pocket with no lining, and ran his finger over the head of his cock.... and collected the receding flow of precum onto his finger. He quickly removed the hand and took the liquid into his mouth. Nothing to waste.

The scents that filled his nostrils were of sex, scandal, doubt, desire, and distracting mixture of homo and heterosexual lust and need. While there are other of his kind who preferred servants of the other sex, the thought of having a female servant left him ill and a tad vacant. He would rather spend a hundred years buried in dirt under the embarcadero, turning and tossing to the rumble of earthquakes than interact with a female as he would need to as with a servant. There were another others who required that type of companionship, that focusing in on men...was much more satisfying and enjoyable. In the end, having the warmth and distinctive scent of a human male with him....was just how he had been born.

He turned his focus back from the past, to the present and the flurry of motion on the platform. He scanned the audience before him and saw many homosexuals, several homosexuals. He noticed the M train was arriving and watched for the members of the crowd moving towards the edge of the platform. Furry ass was one of them. It wasn't until he actually looked in his direction, that Maximillian found the pup staring at him. Once discovered the human diverted his eyes to the train approaching.

Maximillian smiled under his beard. The sharp canine teeth not showing. The hunger growing inside him, not showing either....you couldn't go showing your whole hand so early in the evening.

He watched the pup slip on the train quickly as it arrived. Maximillian strode confidently to the same train and stepped on. Maybe first impressions were good after all. He looked at his watch. 9 pm........

......

......9pm. It was early. Early enough that he knew getting off at Castro Station and heading for Shaft. There would still be some life on the streets. Thursdays were not a large party night, cept for those few who were just letting time pass in the Castro until the club opened.

Marcus had quickly jumped on the train when the leather daddy had noticed him. He normally didn't find men that old attractive, but there was an almost oozing energy coming from that man in leather. He was dressed rather...extreme upon second review. Not many men wore storm trooper coats.... even in the dead of winter; regardless of it being an abnormally cold Halloween. With the wind, it probably felt like the 40s outside, and the wind pouring down from the fog-covered hills wasn't helping any. Marcus has his required standard leather jacket to keep him warm. It had been one of the first things he purchased when moving to San Francisco.

It was one of the only places in the world he knew that could be in the 80s during the day. But once the darkness of night and the blanket of fog arrived, temps could drop very quickly. A good jacket was a necessity... and thankfully being a gay city.... pretty inexpensive.

Van Ness station passed by quickly. Some off. Some on.

Marcus loved taking the MUNI. There were always so many different people on the train. One of the other reasons he loved the city by the bay. Its diversity didn't just apply to the gay community; it was everywhere you looked, if you looked with purpose. Where else in the North America, would you find so many different cultures? Well ok, New York, and maybe Montreal. Marcus had found his love of life here in the city.

More people found themselves on the train and the people around him shuffled. Civic Station would be approaching soon, and Marcus just ran through his goals for the evening. A beer or two at Daddies or Edge, and then it would be off to the club.

It wouldn't be till the doors at Civic Station had closed, till he saw the hard rough boots upon the transit floor standing before him. He couldn't bring himself to look up. He knew who it was...

...The pup seemed lost in thought when he first stood beside him. The pup seemed to be wandering in thoughts. That was till he opened his blue eyes and found Maximillian's boots in their sight. Max surely thought he could see the human tense up. That brought a smile to his face...the human was shy. How cute...how attractive actually.

The human didn't look up. He seemed almost frozen, unable or unwilling to look up. That was when the new scent hit his nostrils. This human was aroused. But the scent coming from him was a very unique and hungry scent. There was submission in this human, in great quantities, coupled with a hunger. This human needed flesh. This human needed rough feeding flesh. The hunger rippled off him like waves towards Maximillian's boots. His cock rose at the strong aroma.

The train came to a stop. The human pup stood, and looked Maximillian in the face. He bowed slightly. Maximillian smiled. He started to say something to the pup, but the boy dashed out of the train. Before the Master knew what had happened, the pup had slipped out of the transit, and the door had closed. Not only had the pup distracted him, he had managed to get off the train, without Maximillian following him.

Now he would have to go all the way to West Portal and travel back to Castro Station.

Now...the pup had done it. The hunt was on.

Part Two

As the train arrived in the West Portal Station, the doors opened and he walked out on to the platform. The scents of seawater, and the city filled his nostrils. He sadly lost the full scent of the human that he had met on the train. He had stood rather stunned, as the train had left Castro Station. It had been a long time since a human had aroused him like this one had. There was that required scent of submission that tinged the sweat and homosexual sweetness that made every bone in his body twitch with hope. There had been too many years since that twitch had rippled through his body before. It was too long.

It wasn't that his kind was immortal. Immortality is a state of being. When one lives 800 years, time has lesser meaning to you. One year to a human could be a lifetime, but to him and his brethren it was a blink. But, he had been reminded of the frailty of time recently.

A month ago, everything had seemed…an eternity. It was always in the places one forgets when time is slower, and gentler. On the eve of his 795th year of life, he found himself wandering the haight district. There were many great times in the 50s, 60s and 70s there. No matter the life in the bay area, it was one of just a few places where he felt like home. Whether the mammoth city of this new age, or the wooden Rick shack of the 1800s, San Francisco, and what the Indians called it before that…would always been one of his homes.

Haight seemed to hold on to the previous age of man. Bookstores, record shops that still carried long playing records. He'll admit to being fascinated with the black discs since back in the day, they were new. The sound they produced was unique. The compact discs and satellite radios of today, had taken away the character of recordings. The record store in the haight was always somewhere he could spend an afternoon rummaging through records. Memories attached to each, some good wondrous dreams, and some devilish nightmares that belonged in the past.

"Maxmillian Trent, looking in the show tunes section, that is not like the Maximillian I remember...." Said the soft toned female voice.

He turned to see the woman standing with a cane. Age had returned to her face, but it was unmistakably Patricia Freist. She was looking good for her age.

"You are well young one...?" She said softly.

Maximillian smiled at the nickname. Back in the years of old, when he was just 145....to her over 300, he was a young one. She had shown him so many things. None of the humans standing in the shop, or even behind the counter would realize that the two figures in the show tunes section, had survived the plague, and three world wars. Maximillian always considered the English American conflict of the late 1700s, the First World War. Some would disagree.

"So you have returned to the Haight.....young one?" the woman asked.

"Actually, I have bought a home up in the river, and I have a small apartment to sleep in while in the city. You know how much I am really not a city boy..."

The woman laughed.

"You were never a boy......born an adult you were...," she said with a wink in her eye.

"You and Charles are in SF now?"

"No actually, Charles had a sight that you would be here...so we came.....to remind you..."

Maximillian frowned.

"I know what you have come to remind me of woman.....you did train me well....I know of your warnings, your protections and your desire for the melancholy, and romantic..."

The woman tapped her cane.

"I might be an old woman now, but you mind your manners Maximill..."

The glimmer of age in her eye and the brief reveal of sharp razor teeth. It was all Maximillian needed to heed the woman.

"You are reaching the age of transformation, you need to find a consort...," Patricia said coldly.

Maximillian flipped through the S section. Showgirls, Showboat, Singing in the Rain.

"You must not enter the age of transformation alone, it is too unbearable to experience alone..." the woman stated with emphasis on the word "alone."

Maximillian flipped the records back and turned to her.

"I have not found the spark in the men of today. You found Charles in the 1800s. When man had spark for adventure...."

Diana smiled when Maximillian mentioned her partner's name.

"How is the old coot doing....now that he has become one...?"

"You pompous little bastard, I am doing fine...," came a clear tenor toned voice.

Two linen covered arms wrapped around his waist. Human warmth basked over Maximillian's back. It was a good feeling.

"And you look good for a man turning 100 soon...." Maximillion laughed.

Maximillian turned to find a thin balding man smiling back at him.

"Mistress knew we had to come...."

The flash of light poured through the man's eyes.

"Mistress Patricia and Charles...it is good to see you both. And yes, my lady I am aware of the coming anniversary. It is one of the reasons I have the small place south of market. I do need to hunt."

Patricia sighed.

"We are both aware, that we cannot find you a suitable replacement for Thomas. That light will never be replenished," the woman said with softness that only their kind could possess, "He was a light that brightened your world, and mine. And all the others who cared for him in his last days."

Maximillian flipped into the R section, Rhapsody in Blue, Robocop. He had been doing well to put Thomas out of his mind. He has spent most of the last 200 years erasing memories. Holding on to only the ones that were needed to smile on starlit nights, and sunsets on unburdened shores. Holding onto only enough to let the memory survive.

Patricia turned to her relative and smiled.

"We did not mean to lecture you, you do not require that type of visit…"

Maximillian smiled and let go of the records.

"No Auntie Patricia…. I don't. I am thankful of your words."

The two older beings then hugged in him unison. The mixture of brethren and human touch was heartwarming. He could feel the two souls of the beings around him. They were filled with love.

"Enough with these discs, I require brunch…and you should know of a good place for a Mistress to have lunch with her nephew and her consort….and who knows we might even find time for Charles…. to interact with you on a more personal nature," she said with a smile.

Maximillian smiled at both of them.

"Yes, I know where there is a lunch that would meet your unique needs and desires. And as for Charles interacting with me on an intimate level…. has he been a good boy?"

The human bowed his head. The Mistress smiled.

"The boy has been very good…."

A slight smile formed on Charles's lips.

"So my young one, off to lunch ……."

SMOKE

That conversation was a year ago Nov.. Patricia and Charles had bought a house in the hills over Oakland. They attended services at the Mormon Temple weekly, and had lunch with Maximillian once a week. Charles sometimes accompanied them both to the Opera, and to the Broadway touring shows. The year of transformation was slowly approaching, and the consort had never appeared...but then was this pup. This human that had the right scent; the scent he had only inhaled from one other human being. Thomas was the only other soul that he had so deeply taken to; where a human's scent alone was reason to fuck him mind body and soul. Where just having the human around gave Maximillian purpose. He needed have that scent in his nostrils again.....before the moonset and the day returned. He needed that human pup...at his feet. He needed to see that human knelt before him. Not necessarily for sexual interaction. Sex to early in the hunt, made things complicated. No....this hunt would be like his last one. Pure. Erotic. Stimulating. Lasting. Bonding.

He closed his eyes and saw Castro Street Station in his mind. When he opened his eyes, he found himself standing in front of the bank, at the top of the stairs, of Castro Station. The crowd of men and woman flying by didn't even see his arrival. Humans rarely could see that much. They were too easily distracted.

If they could they would have seen a man in a storm troopers jacket materialize in the square. By the time he reached the normal human's eyesight he had picked up the cigar from his pocket, and cut the end of it. He lit the cigar and produced large puffs of smoke.

He hoped the human liked smoke. If he was, he was about to get a lot of it.

Part Three

Marcus walked off the train with his heart beating wildly. The man had gotten so close to him. He could still smell the mixture of sweat and leather the man released around his seat on the train. One quick breath was slowly released as the doors closed on the train, and the slightly shocked leathermen faded into the tunnel along with the rest of the passengers of the M Train.

He had to have been a tourist. A man like that would remembered and drooled over from afar many nights if they had crossed paths again. It was the type of man that made Marcus exceptionally shy. If this had been his night to work bar or shine boots at the Shaft, it would have been different. When Marcus was working there was no handsome man that didn't go unnoticed, unpleased, and unpampered. As a bartender that was his job, but Thursday nights were his own night. The type of evening where there was no one to please accept himself. But the same fear that faded away while he was at work, was doubled when it was just him, and a handsome man being inches from his touch. This man on the train was more than that. That storm trooper almost dripped with dominance and attraction towards him. As Marcus reached the air and the street above he took in a deep breath. The crispness of the night air filled his lungs with the cool October air.

He reached into his jacket and pulled out the small cigar. He always preferred the pre-clipped cigars. The short ones with the sweet taste were always his preference. Being 5 ft 6, he always felt foolish with a large cigar in his mouth. Many of his friends joked that the cigar was larger than he was. That was when he found sweets at the local tobacco store. Short jokes were something he was used to, but he also knew how to limit their availability.

The warmth of the cigar contrasted with the cold night air and he smiled. Nothing like a good shot of tobacco to relieve one's nerves and let life return to normal. As he walked down the street, he saw the Café's cleaning up after their day, and closing up shop. That meant it was 9 pm, and a perfect time for a draft at Shaft's, and then on to the evening's main event. The Club.

There were several places that a discerning leatherman could still go for nightly entertainment of the sexual variety. There were still two full-blown bathhouses, one in Oakland, and one in the other side of the bay in San Jose.

Marcus preferred the new version of bathhouse, which of course to the normal observer wasn't a bathhouse at all. There was no shower, there was no pool, and there were no private rooms. The leather clubs provided a space where intimacy and eroticism was created in groups, voyeurism, and the masculine atmosphere of a leather bar. No alcohol was served, but the rest of the leather bar atmosphere would be place.

The Club had different themes each Thursday. There was the underwear night. If one was into briefs. There was the bear night. If you drooled over fur. But for Marcus, there was one night that met all of his basic requirements. Cigar and Piss Night. There were other clubs that offered one or the other, but providing a smoked filled room where he can kneel and drink a man's piss, was the perfect combination to arouse every inch of him. It was his monthly step into another world. Where bitchy patrons on the other side of the bar, landlords wanting rent on the 1st, not the 3rd, and the hustle of the city were left behind.

It was where his inhibitions left him.

That world wasn't open for another hour.

Marcus decided that a beer would be a good way to relax and get ready for a nice evening at the club. He stepped into Daddy's and the bartender waved at him.

"Hey Marcus!......draft?" the man said with a smile.

"You know me too well....." Marcus answered.

The bartender looked at how Marcus was dressed and smiled.

"One doesn't wear untorn Levis, and an ironed yellow hanky in his right pocket, and a shirt that says "Recycle Here"....without me knowing he wants beer to run through him."

"I like to advertise properly...." Marcus said with a laugh.

SMOKE

The bartender was named Andrew. He had been one of the first people that Marcus had met when he arrived in SFO. He was also the person that gave him his nickname, "Pup". He also knew that if Andrew weren't in a 20-year relationship with the owner, they would be a couple. Every other month Marcus would find himself on the receiving end of a night's full of water piss from the bartender. He would drink water all evening, and make to the Club...to feed it to his "Pup." But that was the only extent of their relationship sexually. Andrew's partner didn't want it go further than that. Marcus respected the limits of their interaction. But in the long run it was Andrew's friendship that was more important that the amount of piss that could be fed to him once a quarter.

Andrew had helped him find the job shining boots at Shaft on weekends. The crew at the Shaft had been good to Marcus. Like any bar crew they were a family. Marcus tipped Andrew well, as he noticed the busy bar in front of his best friend.

"Busy night I see...."

"I love cold weather brings all the leather out....makes me feel good inside..."

"You should have seen the guy I saw on the train coming up here....."

Andrew smiled widely.

"Really, Tell Uncle Andy everything..."

Marcus proceeded to tell his friend about the man on the train. How his scent made your skin ripple with anticipation of if that how good he smelled, dear god, how good it would be to taste. How dominant and focused he was. And how...he slipped off the train.

"You should have let him get off with you...." Andrew insisted.

"He was out of my league, I'll probably never see him again..."

Andrew's expression changed.

"I wouldn't be so sure..."

In the doorway to the bar walked the man in the storm trooper jacket.

"Oh he is a handsome one...." Andrew said, but when he turned to see Marcus.... the boy was gone from the chair.

Maximillian stepped to the front of the bar, and hoped for a scent of the boy. He smiled under his beard as he saw the human sitting at the bar talking to the bartender. He had been noticed as the bartender nodded in his direction. The human that had been with him on the train quickly slipped from the chair and into the crowd. Maximillian went to step in the bar with his cigar lit and the bartender quickly came up to him.

"Sorry, we cant smoke those in here anymore..." the bartender said politely.

"Oh..of course..."

Maximillian walked back to the exit. He knocked off the ashes of the cigar, and tapped the cigar out. He placed it in the plastic tube for later use and turned back around. He found the bartender scanning him. Not the feeling that the bartender wished to sleep with him, but more sizing him up. Checking out his stature. It made Maximillian a little nervous and made him chuckle a little.

"If you only knew what you were trying to size up human," he whispered under his breath.

He walked up to the bar and the whole area had the scent of the human from the train.

"I didn't mean to scare your friend off?" Maximillian tried to say in a slight tone.

"Pup is just a shy one..."

Pup huh. So the human has a nickname. A very attractive one considering who was hunting him now.

"You know him?"

"Yeah Marcus and I are old friends..."

"I don't mean him any harm...."

"He might like a little harm…actually. He is a kinky little fucker. But quite the shy one." The bartender offered.

Maximillian was liking him more and more.

"I am Maximillian," he said as he offered his hand to the bartender.

"People call me Pops, but my name is Andrew."

The bartender had relaxed. Good. He didn't need a human interrogating him about past and interests. He just wanted a beer and hoped the human "Pup" would come back by him.

"What will it be Maximillian?"

"An Ale, your best," the brethren male answered.

Maximillian watched in the mirror behind the bar as the human pup slipped by him and towards the door. The ale was laid before him. The bartender smiled.

"He goes to the CLUB on Thursdays, specially this one…." The bartender said with a sly smile.

"The Club?"

"His favorite place to play…"

"Ah, a sexual place…"

"The only one he'll go to. It's Cigar and Piss night. You seem to enjoy one of the fetishes…" the bartender continued to offer.

Maximillian flashed his best human smile at the bartender.

"Cigars are just the beginning of my 'fetishes' Andrew…"

The bartender swallowed and then said he had other customers.

"Enjoy your evening…."

The bartender moved on to other men with cash in their hand, needing a beer or more strong drinks. Maximillian smiled once again as he saw the human pup standing at the door watching him.

The human pup did like smoke. Good. It was just many of the things he would be feeding him that evening. With that thought, the human pup slipped from the doorway back into the city.

After a slow drink of ale, Maximillian would follow.

The hunt would continue. And like a good bottle of wine, it was getting better with time.

Part Four

There are moments that a piano can sound like a heartbeat. They are sounds that are like a race of notes, rather than melody, lying below the recognizable, and staying out of the focus. But, if the music is clever enough, and the melody entrancing, you will forget all about the other notes beneath and fall in love with song up above.

There were times the world around Maximillian was that heartbeat. That race that he didn't belong in. it hadn't always been that way, and as he found himself walking through the streets south of Market his memory blurred. His mind wandered through times when life seemed to be endless. Walking through the mountains of what was now Yellowstone National Park, laughing with friends how humans in Europe would never understand this part of the world. How the folk that inhabited the North Americas now.... were a more natural type of human. They both understood where the brethren stood in the world, and where humans should stand as well. He remembered standing on the edge of the Grand Canyon with many Indians around him, reveling its majesty and the many mysteries that lay beneath the rim of the massive canyon and the angry river that lived in the bottom. It was also in this wilderness he first found the touch of a human pleasing. Over 300 years had passed since those simpler days. San Francisco was a thriving metropolis and the world before it a distant memory, and only something told in history books to the humans.

For Maximillian, the city had regenerated itself into a new playground.

Death did that. It took places that were intolerable in the last century and provided new joys.

Death was something he was used to. It occurred around the brethren all the time. It was one of the reasons his people almost never interacted with humans on an emotional intense basis. For just as you got to know one, and know the warmth of their touch and the love in their heart, they passed away. Leaving you alone to grieve. Most brethren mated with their species and found love in the outer barriers of human life. Discrete, but nevertheless satisfying. Certain people could tell that they were different. But most humans, the ones that could never see Maximillian materialize were numbered in the hundreds of thousands, but when you find one that can....it can be a miracle or a disease. The brethren had an agreement with seers. Humanity on a whole cannot understand what is watching over them. They could not bare the knowledge that something was higher on the food chain....he chuckled at that thought....humans were afraid of werewolves and the boogey man. Many of the brethren left the seers alone, but Maximillian and his lineage were different. They were the communicators. The link between humans and the other creatures of this earth that were different. Brethren weren't the only immortal type creatures. Angels hadn't been to Earth for a millennia. They had long ago found a new state of being. Children wouldn't probably sleep at night knowing things like werewolves, vampires, mummies and such lived among them. It was better that way. Through Seers, the communities lived in harmony since before Christ walked the Earth as the last Angel of God to come to Earth.

But that was all in the past.

Maximillian found himself lost in these thoughts as the darkened streets of San Francisco led him to "THE CLUB". And now...he found himself entranced by a human again. Of course there were more things at stake than just the lust and heat two bodies could form. Now....there was the longing of fulfillment and the end of the waiting. The scent of the human was still fresh in his palette. The sweat in the mixture was quite alluring. He wanted to add to that scent. Thankfully there was a myriad of ways to make the pup's scent, identifiable to him uniquely. He planned on some of the more enjoyable ones in good time.

Humans were frail in some ways. He wondered about the aging process, and how...60 felt. To have your body slowly slow down from the moment 60 years of age finds you. He was always jealous when he found a friend at that age. Soon enough he would feel it, but he needed to bond first.

"You need to find a human to bond with, and to feed from. Not just their heat during passion, but a human that can feed you outside the passion of sexual interaction, and warm your changing heart....and keep it warm ways neither of you can imagine.." Patricia had said.

All Brethren are taught of the transformation from near immortal to human, and how it was important to have a guide. To have bonded with

someone so that when age begins, the new world is entered into with someone to be with them. Maximillian would enter the year of transformation in
almost a year. Bonding would take at least that long. He hoped this new
pup was eager. There was a sexual hunger trickling off his skin, almost like
unseen syrup. He wanted to taste that syrup and bathe in it.

He clipped a new fresh cigar and stepped through the front door.
The blast of human testosterone that hit him was almost blinding. What was
this place....? He asked himself.

"ID please," the scruffy man at the counter asked.

"Oh, you want a one time, or a year membership."

Maximillian looked up at the neatly printed sign showing the options
of membership to "THE CLUB". Since it seemed the pup liked it there, a
year membership made the most sense. Soon a shiny plastic covered card
with Maximillian's signature and a metal like writing "CLUB" on it was
returned to him.

"Come on in, I'll show you round....you seem new to a place like
this?..." the scruffy man greeted.

Maximillian nodded. The sexual tension in the air almost over-
whelmed him. Every hair on his body was shifting in the tides of lust. He
stepped through the door as a buzzer seemed to release the latch on the
door and he found himself in a sort of make shift locker room. The scruffy
man reappeared.

"Master Maximillian, we have never seen you here before...." The
scruffy man said softly.

The Brethren's wit returned to him. He stared into the scruffy man's
eyes to see a familiar shine brighten inside. This large scruffy man was a
Seer. He was quite an experienced one from the aura that spilled around
him. Especially since he seemed to know who Maximillian was.

"How do you know of me, young one?" Maximillian answered softly.

"Well you're the only Master who wears a coat like yours. It is a
trademark of yours, and of the few sightings...we have had...when Andrew
from the bar called to let me know a "stranger" (he lifted his hands to make
quotations, humans were so funny like that)....and he described you....this

servant knew of your approach. Most Brethren don't come here, I am told it is an intense experience," the man answered.

Maximillian was working hard to keep his composure.

"Males come here for non strings, no nonsense sex. Wolves come here a lot, just when in heat, to have their cocks sucked for hours, one or two brethren come here, but they come with their companions.... it is quite an honor..."

Maximillian lifted his hand to shush the man.

"I need to remove my coat, the experience has raised my warmth quite well...."

The Seer put out his hands to receive his jacket. The scruffy almost gasped when he removed the jacket to reveal nothing was worn underneath but a full body metal harness, with his family's seal embedded in the metal.

"You find something distasteful?" he asked.

The seer turned and put Maximillian's coat on a hanger. He chuckled.

"On the contrary, Master Maximillian."

"Oh dear lord, call me max, young one. Enough with the rules of engagement."

The scruffy man visibly relaxed.

"You are a very handsome brethren, men will flock to you for pleasure..."

Max smiled at the comment. There were many years that a 6 ft 2 man with a muscular build, inches of dark black fur, large nipples, and a hefty manly cock larger than most, would have both man and woman rejecting him. Thank god times had changed.

The Seer seemed to be scanning him quietly.

"I believe the modern expression is, if you have a web cam I'll give you a tour..."

The scruffy doorman quickly shifted the conversation.

"You are searching for the one named Marcus SIR?"

There was stiffening in Max's demeanor.

"Yes, the one named Marcus..."

"He'll be a floor down, the watersports room is open..."

Maximillian smiled very wide, and revealed the entire set of teeth to the Seer. The Seer seemed in awe. Maximillian stepped forward to the human Seer and wrapped his arms around him, covering the short man in his fur and arms. The Seer relaxed and almost went limp.

"You have done well servant, very well indeed. You should know it has been many cycles since I have fully released....your clientele here is in for quite a night."

He released the Seer who was visibly aroused.

"You are going to release here...with the other humans present, MASTER?" the Seer said with an almost hungry grin.

"That would be correct...."

"How much time do I have?"

Maximillian smiled.

"An hour at maximum..."

"At your service SIR."

The scruffy man walked to the counter to his co-worker with a large smile.

"We are going to make a lot of money off the snacks, we are going to have a very hungry crowd in about two hours ...btw. If you don't have poppers, get some handy.... this is going to a great night!"

"What's going on Boss, he's cute but he aint that cute...?" the attendant said softly.

"Trust me …you'll thank me later.."

Maximillian walked into the club and let the energy ripple off him. The warmth of two lovers fucking like rabbits in the sling to his left, the smell of warm pipe and cigar smoke filling the air, and the older man getting orally serviced by two men on their knees. The man nodded at Max with a wide smile.

He came to the top of the steps and felt a days worth of piss coming up within him. The ale had put him over that edge. It was time to find the pup and start his first night of learning the pup. He hoped the pup would be receptive. Soon, someone would have to feel his release, and not just his release of piss.

Marcus lay in the bathtub, being slightly disappointed at the attendance in the piss room. One-man pity party, no appetizers. That all changed when the dominant man appeared at the top of the stairs. Although, there was no storm trooper jacket, it was quite obvious who was walking down the stairs towards him. Marcus couldn't move, as he looked this man over. He was a giant, and jesus the fur on his body. He was a walking carpet. (Check, in the good column), his cock was uncut and hung quite easily beyond 9 inches (check), the nips on his chest looked like not only did they like being chewed on it, it was demanded (check). And his gloves….he hadn't removed the gloves (check check check).

The man was now standing in front of the tub. He smiled as he released a puff of smoke from the cigar (Check).

"Do you wear piss well pup?" the man asked.

OH DEAR GOD FUCKING RIGHT I LIKE TO WEAR PISS, I'D WEAR YOURS IN THE MIDDLE OF GODDAMN BLOOMINGDALES….was what Marcus thought.

"Yes SIR," he answered audibly.

"You wish to earn it?"

This guy was good. Marcus gulped.

"Stand."

Marcus delayed.

"Don't make me ask twice. I don't like being kept waiting."

Marcus stood. He stared into the man's eyes. Dark grey eyes that showed intensity he hadn't felt before.

"You don't look down?" the voice asked of him.

He immediately diverted his eyes.....to the boots the man was wearing. A gloved hand moved up to his chin.

"I like you looking at me, Puppy...don't stop..."

Marcus was now fully aroused. As if trying to see how turned on he could make Marcus, the man lifted an arm revealing that the dark hair covered the armpit. The scent coming from his pit was enough to Marcus drool.

"Do you like eating armpits?"

Marcus immediately said yes. The man's accent was quite a nice touch; he was foreign (CHECK!). The glove left his chin and swiftly grabbed the back of his head shoving him into the hairy armpit.

"Eat..."

Marcus gorged on the fur and the scent. It was quite intoxicating.

The arm was lowered.

"Good boy, you have earned the right to wear my piss, now that you have my scent on that beard of yours..."

Marcus stood dumbfounded.

"Kiss me....pup."

They lip locked.... roughly, both of their saliva dripping between their bodies. The man just as roughly pulled away again.

"Back into your tub with you…"

Marcus returned to his laid back position.

"I think you are going to like this a lot.." the man said with a soft smile.

The piss poured out of the uncut cock all over his body. It poured like gushes, like the man hadn't pissed in hours. He reached up and worked his eraser size nipples as the gush continued. He smiled wider revealing large white almost polished teeth. The piss kept flowing in controlled bursts from the gloved hand controlling the flow out of his cock.

"Wear my piss well, Pup…"

"Oh yes SIR."

The two males locked eyes….and Marcus wasn't afraid anymore.

Not afraid of this man at all.

Part Five

Marcus lay in the covers of his bed, letting the sunshine fall upon the bedroom. Normally he would have ran for the covers and hid from the light of day. There were so many weekdays spent wandering the streets of the city, watching life go by. These were times where he would pull the blinds and let it go on without him. Life outside in the daylight only brought pain and anguish. Pain and frustration that he didn't need in his life; so he hid from it. This morning was very different…. from many others lately. He wanted to mingle under the covers and enter the daylight with a smile. He flipped the business card in his fingers, the writing rotating in and out of view. "Maximillian Trent, 1870 Fell, 415/555-9855 For a boy who deserves more of my time"

He had never met anyone who spoke like the man from the night at the club. There was an antiquity about him. Oh god, and the accent had driven him mad. Normally all it took was a strong accent and Marcus was aroused. This man could read the side of a box of children's cereal and he would be turned on. But his voice had nothing to his touch.

The club had been relatively empty up till then. Just as it was getting busy, and he hadn't begun to get wet, the man appeared at the top of the stairs. The pure and simple dominance that poured from the man made Marcus drool from all places you could.

The warmth of his piss when it started to pour gave him all of Marcus's attention. The boy loved it when a man had stored up lots of piss, came to the club, and chose him to soak. Because he had seen him earlier on the subway, the attraction was also mixed with some acknowledgement of his shyness around the man earlier. But being naked in a tub covered in piss as the man walked down the stairs, did quite well removing the barriers of shyness that normally plagued him.

The man had walked right up to him. No one distracted him, not even the muscle boys that were in his wake, looking at the furry muscle with just as much admiration as Marcus had. The muscle bear leather master daddy wanted Marcus. He wouldn't complain. Most of the piss poured over his chest, down around his hardened cock and pooled under his balls near his ass. It was a warm welcoming bath of urine, that Marcus got only once or twice in an evening. When the piss dribbled to drops falling on his chest, the leather glove handed man took a gentle but noticeable grasp on the back of his head.

"You aren't done yet, young man." The voice informed.

Marcus saw the dribble of piss forming on the foreskin.

"Drink...."

Marcus obeyed. The foreskin revealed a large pisshead, which once within his mouth a last gush of piss poured in. Marcus almost didn't swallow fast enough to adapt. The piss upon his tongue was strong and beer flavored. The warm fluid slid down his throat, and he wanted more. Oh god did he want more. The cock in his mouth began to harden, and the hand wasn't letting him go either. He looked up at the man's eyes. It was a position that he loved being in. His throat wrapped around this Daddy's cock, not sucking...more suckling....keeping it warm and drippy with his saliva.

"If you suck that cock boy, don't expect me to let you stop till I cum. But you won't swallow my cum tonight. You'll wear it home. Do you under-stand me...when I release you head and say pull back...do so. DO NOT SWALLOW."

The man pulled his cock out of Marcus's warm mouth.

"Answer...."

"Yes SIR."

Marcus looked down at the tub again.

"Never answer looking down at the floor.... always answer looking into my eyes, do you understand both of the things I tell you pup?"

Marcus shivered as the piss started to cool on his body.

"Yes SIR," he said as he raised his eyes to meet the dark grey eyes of the daddy before him.

"Good. Now get out of the tub. Someone else needs to get wet, you and I are getting comfortable...."

The look on the boy's face when he told him to get out of the tub was purely piggy. He loved seeing the slight confusion on the human's face as he was told to get out of the tub. Almost as if saying "But what if someone wants to piss."

That was when he said. "Someone else might want to get wet, we … are getting comfortable…"

After little afterthought, the naked human obeyed him. It made his cock stir. Preventing his feeding of cum to this human before other interaction was going to be hard to do at best. The human was worth investigating and learning more. He was looking for a willing servant, not a forced one. They would date. Something Patricia would not understand completely, but would come to accept. The thought of courting this handsome little furball turned him on, as he took the human by the neck....massaging as they walked....searching for the perfect place to truly introduce the boy to his cock.

They walked the halls, the human saying nothing. Just watching the room around them. He could see the boy's cock was at full attention. He would enjoy milking it completely dry. Watching the human writhe as his gloved hands relieved him of his load. It would be wonderful to see how this particular man reacted at that moment.

They came around a corner to a small room with a large chair lifted on a platform, and it was inset into the wall. There was a red light above the chair. They would be on display…. perfect.

Maximillian let go of the pup's neck, and sat in the chair. He pointed to his hard dripping cock, pulled back the sheath of foreskin and smiled.

"EAT…"

The boy did not disappoint him. He had found as he had hoped an expert human submissive. One with experience to swallow even the length of Maximillian's larger cock was hard to find. This boy was having no problem swallowing all 10 inches and leaving it drenched in deep throat human juices. He would have cum in his beard very soon, and lots of it.

Maximillian drew his cigar, lit it, and began puffing large puffs down at the pup. If anything the smoke made the boy suck better...deeper...with an aggression and hunger. The warmth started to fill Maximillian. As the boy continued to bring the Brethren closer and closer to climax, he was oblivious to what was happening around him. He focused on the cock in his throat. Only Maximillian could watch men start having sex with others. There was no one standing alone. In groups of two, three and even more, the men in the club were all fucking. There was only one who was not. It was the Seer, the owner of the club. He stood with his cock in his hand on the far side of the club, but within seeing distance of Maximillian. He was stroking his cock in his hand, and Maximillian could sense he was holding back. No one else was. The seer was ready, and had been a good host.

Max felt the warmth break from his skin, and down across the human on his cock. The wave hit the human and his sucking doubled in intensity. This was going to be a large feeding of emotion, the boy would be covered in cum once Maximillian released what was inside.

Maximillian watched as the wave of emotion and lust, and its warmth burst over the couples. The fucking getting harder, the sucking going deeper, the kissing increasing in the passion of the moment. As the wave hit the Seer, the brethren smiled as the Seer came in big white globs of cum. Maximillian then shouted, "PULL AWAY."

The boy obeyed.

Within second big white sheets of cum splattered the humans face and chest. A second wave splashed through the club. With a white hot flame, that only the brethren could see.... orgasms hit all in the room and the white flame then retreated from them and focused on the human between his legs.

Inside his mind Maximillian just said one simple word..."CUM."

The boy shuddered as cum spilled forth on to Marcus's legs and boots. The tremble in his face as he couldn't stop his cum from releasing from his balls. The human shot quite far, and all over Marcus's boots.

"You have cum on my boots."

Without even Maximillian finishing the sentence, the boy leaped to his boots and started removing the cum. All through the facility...once could hear men cumming, shooting, and recovering from cumming. The scent of male satisfaction filled Maximillian's nostrils.

He rubbed the back of the boy's head as he moved to the second boot.

Maximillian sat in his study reading the morning paper, several hours later and saw the pair of boots..in the corner that the boy had been licking so hungrily. He stepped up to them and breathed in their scent. The boy's ejaculation was still ingrained in the boots. Maximillian grabbed a hold of his cock and stroked.

As the stream of cum flew through the air, landing on the carpet…Maximillian was sure of one thing. He hoped the boy would call, and the hunt would continue.

Part Six

Several Months Later

Maximillian could spend hours with this human being. It fathomed him the emotions he had began to bring out in him, in just the month that they had started interacting. The pup called it "dating". It had begun with a simple walk along the pier, and laughing over an order of fried potatoes strips. The young man had manners, and truly wanted to be around him. He wasn't ashamed of being around other people and showing emotion towards Maximillian. It was something that made his heart warm inside. The walks were turning into afternoons at the movies, followed by several hours of passionate kissing and fondling. It was truly…. bringing out new feelings and warmth. He now found himself at a crossroads. The human pup had asked for him to spend the night. To sleep with him, not just for a nap, but overnight.

He resisted at first. There were barriers that one got used to being around his heart. They had been around him for so long….that when the human started knocking at them he found himself wanting to keep them up, but his allure prevented him from sticking to his guns. The pup was reaching to inner emotions now. It wasn't just his touch that made him melt it was his manners, his smile, his gentleness and most of all his submissiveness. Maximillian sat in his study and once again found himself staring at the pair of boots that had started all this. This time they were not….scuffed, scratched….they were shiny, buffed and reflective. The pup shined them. "There they look like new!" He didn't need to be told they were over 100 years old. That would have ruined it all.

Maximillian had known that the pup shined boots at one of the local watering holes on weekends, so the past Saturday night he walked to the bar. He hadn't told Marcus that he would be outside waiting after work, or come by when you are done. The Brethren needed the hunt aspect to arise once in a while. Something gentle to remind the human who was in charge.

The scents of human males filled the room, with the after hints of deodorant (which was despicable),,,or even worse the slight hint of cologne (disgusting)…but thankfully his pup worked in a bar that discouraged both.

This was a masculine setting for the human to work in. It also was an interesting way to reinforce his need to be submissive. For he was the boy of the crew....the bartenders were called Daddy by most who worked there...and the owner was "boss". They all had a kindred spirit, but Maximillian enjoyed how even the most tattooed buff bartender always seemed to call him SIR when he came in the bar.

He stepped to the edge of the bar scanning the dimly lit scene for the pup. If Marcus had come close enough, the scent would overpower him, and the human would never be lost among all these other males again.

"Your regular draft Max?" the bartender offered.

Maximillian turned his gaze to the bartender. "That would fine..." he said with a gentle smile.

The bartender tipped the front of his leather cowboy hat and fetched the ale. Maximillian then returned to the room of men moving around, hunting each other sexually, and responding to the ever-present beat of the music. Marcus had said it was "fuck music" ...Maximillian had never liked the term. But humans always had the tendency to cheapen the desire and warmth of interaction. One shouldn't even bring up the idea of Valentines Day. It was a holiday created for chocolate, nothing more.

His distraction of the scene soon faded as the short furball appeared from the back storeroom and dropped a case of ale bottles on the bar. He didn't look up, yelled something at the bartender and walked back through the door. A tall glass of ale slid in front of him.

"Anything else you need SIR?"

"Is pup shining tonight....?"

"Oh yeah, as soon as he brings another case he'll be back, he has a sign up board."

Maximillian tipped the bartender over the normal fee for ale, and walked towards the board. A simple chalkboard was hung by the wall, and there were two names scribbled on it. Then the scent filled his nostrils. The human's scent was everywhere. The seat, the wall, the floor, and even the cloths at the foot of the chair....was covered in Marcus sweet accent. Max gritted his teeth and gained control. Splashing the whole bar with a wave of orgasm would probably be good for business, but it would also draw attention where it didn't need to be. He slowly picked up the chalk and wrote on the blackboard. The hardening cock in his leather pants dripped as he wrote. He knew that the pup would like what he saw. He put the chalk down and returned to his ale at the bar.

"You are going to let pup shine your boots..He'll have a fit," the bartender said with a smile.

"Boots are just the start Andrew, my boy, just the start…he is going to shine every bit of me…and he'll earn his tip…"

Maximillian smiled, as the bartender was noticeably aroused as he went to assist other patrons. What Maximillian didn't expect, was that two other names meant he wasn't the first customer that his human companion would serve in the evening. Watching the man he wished to bond with, to make his submissive….would have to serve others in front of him. It would be an evening that many emotions would surface. It was only 9 pm.

……

Marcus had a belief system…and it was that boot blacking wasn't just…shining boots it was much more than that. He believed it as what he called the Tao of Boot Blacking.

Some consider sex, a sexual act involving intercourse, or oral pleasure. Boot blacking provides sexual pleasure in an ornate way. There is lots of oral pleasure involved (well at least there should be). For the receiver of a bootblack's worship, it is a mental stimulation that amounts to orgasm (well, at least it should be.)

The actual act of shining a boot is pretty easy; any child could do it. Being a bootblack and worshipping a pair of boots, is much different. This isn't just shining a pair of boots in the lobby of an international airport and getting a person on its way, so you can rush through another person. It is not about making money, although there are other tips from experience are well worth the effort to receive. Above Marcus's chair was a simple Dark black 6. When people asked, it was for his six rules of boot blacking.

He then turned to his roster of service for the evening. The chalkboard was full of names. He scanned the list, and froze. The third name read "Daddy." Marcus swallowed hard and turned towards the bar….trying to see if he could see Maximillian in the crowd. He then noticed the many rings that Max had lovingly placed around his balls were tightening. The many aggressive rings had been tugging at his balls for several hours now…making his cock a drippy precum covered mess. Seeing the word Daddy on his chalkboard wasn't going to help matters. It made the rings tighten as his balls found the idea of licking his new Daddy's boots in public highly arousing. But being a submissive towards Maximillian poured out of Marcus much easier than with others. It wasn't just the warmth that seemed to fill him when they were interacting sexually. Max was intelligent, articulate, and knew how to adapt to good and bad days. He was also the type of Daddy that gave into the boy once in a while. There was a time when Marcus thought all Daddies had become "all about me" men. Maximillian was something different. They had talks over dinner about life, love and the future. It seemed brighter with this man around. They had also talked about his boot blacking, and that Maximillian didn't necessarily understand how he enjoyed it. That was how the 6 had come into reality.

"Rule #1. What Boot blacking is, is becoming submissive to the leather person who sits upon your chair. It is separating your attentions from other things around you, and becoming infatuated with the pair of leather shoes, boots, and yes, even heels that are presented to you. It is becoming a slave to the leather that has proudly been presented to you by the person in the chair. It is the trust someone gives you when they release the ownership of their leather to your touch, your tongue, and yes, your lust," Marcus had told him.

......

Marcus had never met a man who truly understood what it meant to want to be a man's boy. Maximillian not only knew what it meant but seemed to hold it in great regard. There was genuine interest in his eyes, instead of the normal glazing over. But the feeling was mutual. Marcus loved learning the new ways to please him. The way to arrive at his doorstep with the right cup of coffee, even if that meant getting it in the Castro and taking the MUNI and working hard at "no drips" while the tram jerked its way over the hill to Max's house. It was simple pleasures that seemed to make his new Daddy brim over with appreciation and touch.

It was just that touch that seemed to make Marcus's world shine brighter. He had finally found a man who was quite capable of tying him up, working over his nipples till they were sore, pound his throat with cock, feed him more furry ass than he had fed upon……in years yet, couple that interaction with a gentle intimacy afterwards. There was a level of touch he had never experienced. It was almost if the man would be incomplete without Marcus being in touch with him physically. The Sunday paper had become an intertwined mess of flesh and print.

Marcus's first customer walked up to the chair and sat down in the bootblack station. Max started to get up, and then settled back into his chair. The waiting wasn't going to be easy. The bartender noticed his restlessness.

"You've never seen pup at work before....don't worry. No matter what you see.....his balls are being reminded...about you often." Andrew said.

Maximillian smiled. The rings were doing their job.

"He seemed to like the idea at the time," Maximillian said with a gentle laugh.

"We'll see if he still feels that way at Midnight when he goes home with you..."

Maximillian turned to see his pup shake hands with the first customer. The man was wearing fatigues and lace up boots. They didn't look in half bad condition. It was a time he wished he could sensor his hearing and listen to the conversation they were having. He chuckled to himself that in reality that they could be talking about the latest movie, or last night's television.

Both were a pre-occupation of the human that was now washing off the man's boots. Watching the handsome furball transform was a joy to watch. The conversation had been replaced with a passion to please the pair of boots that were in front of him. It meant the boy was working hard to apply rule #2.

"Rule #2. What Boot blacking is, is taking the simple act of shining leather into the sexual arena that has a mental climax like no other. It is worshipping the person's boots in a submissive way. A way only a bootblack can. It is a turn on while others in the bar or the gathering are watching this submissive transformation take place. It is the changing of a pushy aggressive boy who always wants it his way (you know who you are), to a submissive mental state that there is only one goal, pleasure on behalf the person in your boot blacking chair. All others matters no longer exist..."

If he had learned anything about this pup, is he remembered a lot of things. He called them mental notes. Maximillian had always told the boy from the beginning of their interaction....when he heard Rule #2 something specific.

"That means you'll apply that rule, even if I am in the room watching," he had said. The boy was doing just that. Focusing on the man in the chair. Removing the laces, head down, making the man's cock harden. Submissiveness always effected a good dominant of any race, but when Marcus poured it on...it was more than just simple "yes SIR" ... it was human surrendering his surroundings to please. No matter who was there. The dripping of Maximillian's cock was still a steady drip. There would be a meal there for a deserving boy later in the evening. It was now 10 pm. He was seeing his human pup in his natural environment and he found himself entranced, unable to look away. Even at the young pups that once in a while cruised him, and wanted to drift his attention away from Marcus. They were not succeeding.

Then something happened that made Maximillian whisper "good boy" under his breath. Marcus crouched and licked the freshly shined boots of the man in the chair. He never expected Rule #3 to affect him so much.

Rule #3 was Marcus's favorite part actually. "Rule #3. What Boot blacking is, is the application of your tongue to a pair of boots. Tasting the leather and where it's been. Closing your eyes and becoming a saliva machine, a tongue can provide great pleasure. It is the feeling of a man's hand on your head as you travel over the surface of the boots with hunger. It is taking pride in once you withdraw however brief, your spit has covered every inch of the leather. It glistens in the light."

Marcus knew there were some who figured that they best sexual organ was their cock. While he would agree his cock was a lot of fun, he was sure his tongue brought much more pleasure to his customers....and especially to his daddy. The man was very appreciative of the application of tongue. Marcus had always been glad for a long wet tongue. If he had done his job right.....all he would taste is clean shiny leather. For the first customer, he had. He was tipped well, and the second customer approached.

He reached up with the chalk and scratched out the first name. One name left, till Daddy was in his chair. The second customer was one he had served before....and knew this would really get Daddy going. This customer liked a much more submissive bootblack. He winked at Marcus as he got into his chair, and said deeply "Your Daddy is next pup, shine your boss's boots, and we'll make him want to fuck you right here in the bar, before you're done."

SMOKE

When the lights of the bar went down and the red light above the boot chair brightened, Rule #4 took over. Marcus knew what was coming. It was time to put on a show. It was how the Boss liked it.

He knelt before the owner of the bar and the licked the stale beer from the boots.

He stayed on his knees, and lit the boot wax. The flame danced in his eyes and flicked in an angry flame between the two pairs of boots. It was drawing a crowd. His Boss smiled from above. He wouldn't see Maximillian get off his barstool and start walking through the crowd. He wouldn't stop and look either. After all, Bootblack is a presentation.

"Rule #4. What Boot blacking is is presentation. It is putting polish on the boots with your hands, not a brush. A brush is for those who shine boots in airports, (not a bad profession, just not the one a bootblack in SM is made for). It is lighting the polish on fire, and using a small cloth to apply it. It is putting the polish on in little circles. (You might be thinking of wax on, wax off from Karate Kid, but I wouldn't recommend telling that part to the leather folk that provide you with their boots)."

Watched the flame dance between the owners legs, and the pup almost going into a trance aroused Maximillian even more. He had to get closer. He wanted to see pup go to work. He knew it would be an excellent show. He worked his way to corner of the bar and watched all the men some more interested in the pool game, and the other men than his pup shining boots. He could see others however, that saw the eroticism in a boy on his knees. The flame was now extinguished and the fingers were running the warm liquid wax over the tall boots, and working into the fabric. Maximillian walked around to other end of the bar, and was offered the stool by a familiar face. The bartender was anticipating his move.

"Front row seat…" the man said with a large smile.

Maximillian turned and returned his eyes to the red-lit scene. The boy was working his way up the tall lace less boots. Massaging each inch with the layer of black polish. It almost made Maximillian want to pull the man out, get in his boots, and take his place. The advantage of dating such a handsome submissive creature was that soon the dating would succumb to something deeper and he would have a bootblack with him…at his call. He would also have a man of skill in his command. This human worked up a nightly sweat shining boots. The brethren could still remember the nights of sweat the boy had provided him with. Especially after Maximillian had told to never shower after a night at the bar, that the sweat he dripped into his ass and pits, was his Daddy's reward for the boy being gone. Tonight would be no different.

"He's watching you boy, time to make him remember rule #5."

Marcus grinned up his boss with an absolute evil grin. "Rule #5. What Boot blacking is is something that takes practice. It takes time to polish a pair of boots to the point where you can see your face in them. It takes time for people to appreciate your craft, and know your ability. It takes time to learn to press your tongue against a boot so hard, that they feel it inside. It takes time to know how much pleasure it gives someone to have a boot-black worshipping his or her leathers."

It was the Boss. Harley Stevens. That had shown Marcus where the 6 rules came from. A simple piece of paper that a bootblack had written at a leather convention several years ago was the agreement that Harley and Marcus had come to. If the young handsome man followed those rules, he would be the bootblack here for many years to come. He was a young muscular submissive. A true boy, and one he had wanted sexually at first. But first rule of being a bar owner, never sleep with your staff. The boy had really taken to the rules like a good boy did. His craft was improving all the time. He now had regulars to the point, that when Marcus took his one Saturday night off a month, people sighed in sadness when the boy wasn't there to take care of their boots. The arrival of this new Daddy only made his employee work harder. He could feel Marcus's hands massaging the leather and working really hard. The beads of sweat dropping from his forehead upon the boots, was really made feeding boots to this boy a joy. He really got off on it. It wasn't just a procedure, the boy truly loved boots.

Maximillian was sitting on the stool watching the whole proceeding, as if just watching his boy serving the owner, was arousing in its own degree. Harley did feel his cock pressing against his pants. He didn't know what it was about this new Daddy that was different than the others that tried to court young Marcus. This one wanted it to be a long lasting interaction. Harley was happy with the boy on all counts, he had become a good member of his family.

Marcus stared up from the now shiny boots panting and smiling. As usual, the scruffy pair of chippewas. He was amazed on how scruffy they actually got. Harley had really made sure they were in desperate need of touch up. He looked up at his Boss and he was smiling. There was also a wet spot in his jeans. Marcus must have really worked hard.

"Crawl and fetch your Daddy's boots...."

Marcus turned and found his Daddy sitting on a stool almost directly behind him. There was a glimmer of a smile through the thick goatee of his Daddy. That smile of "oh. How I am going to feed you later....."

Marcus took the Boss's offer and started to crawl towards his Daddy's boots. He never left eye contact with Maximillian. The electricity of their bond left off his skin as he approached the military style lace ups that his daddy wore. He looked up at his Daddy's face and they both smiled.

"I believe you are next SIR?" Marcus inquired.

Maximillian stood up. "I don't know if their dirty enough for you?" Maximillian answered.

Only Marcus knew that the only softening of the shine on the boots was the cum the two men had been placing on them for the past two days while he had been off work. Only Daddy would understand what he did next.

Marcus slid forward and ran his tongue over each boot...from toe to the tied laces at the top. Harley looked on from the boot chair, adding more wetness to his pants, as he adjusted his now hard cock...and stepped out of the boot chair.

Maximillian smiled down at the human.

"Well, when you put it that way, boy, how can I resist your charm...?"

He stepped up in the chair, and watched the owner of the bar grabbing another boy in the crowd by the back of the neck. As Marcus knelt before his Daddy, Maximillian watched the owner of the bar lean against the far back dark wall of the club. The top half of the man disappeared into other darkness along with the boy he took with him dropping to his knees. And into the darkness.

He looked down at Marcus who continued to lick at the boots.

The boy stopped...and smiled.

"Thank you Daddy."

"No thank you boy…thank you."

Maximillian knew there was a rule #6, but for now all that mattered was the handsome pup between his legs, lighting the boot wax. The flare of fire dancing in his eyes, and the submissiveness washing over him again, made the dance of fire even more arousing. Soon, more would be revealed to his pup, and the time for decisions would be made. He didn't know how much longer he could hold back feeding this human his seed. There would be no turning back once true feeding began. But for this night, he watched his pup massage the polish into the boots. There would be other nights soon enough for talks of times past, and the longer future ahead.

Part Seven

Marcus was beginning to love the moments when his Daddy's piss was still fresh on his tongue. When the hint of where he had been was on his flesh, and what he drank was fresh in his piss, were the times the Marcus not only made himself happy but also made his new Daddy even more proud of him. Maximillian Trent had an appointment for the afternoon and had left the boy at Marcus's appointment with a full gut of Daddy piss. He said to be ready by 8 pm. He was to be dressed in slacks, and a nice shirt. There were people to meet this evening, which were important to Maximillian. Two of his oldest friends he had said lifting up his fingers to create quotation marks. His thick European accent turning minutely southern as he tried to imitate a southerner's voices when he said "oldest" and it brought a smile to Marcus's face. Patricia and Clive were people that Max had spoken of often, but never actually introduced Marcus to them. He knew that this evening would be important.

What he did know of Patricia and Clive was a mixed bag of information. Patricia was his Aunt. Clive was her second husband, and they were both in their 60s. Maximillian said that the evening would be full of adventure and surprise, and that his loving boy should be ready for anything.

"Anything. Well…that left many things up in the air didn't it," Marcus thought.

The two men had spent the morning running errands. They had stopped by the upper floor Tower Records, where Maximillian had enjoyed watching Marcus fly through the rows, finding music, and introducing him to new sounds. From the looks of Max's CD collection, if it is wasn't written in the 1700-1800s it didn't exist. Slowly the boy introduced new things to his collection. Today…..they had purchased a collection. Marcus quite enjoyed laying the man's arms as his stereo filled the morning lit living room with music and the laughter of his Daddy's chest, as they listened to Ladies Who Lunch. Another gay man was now a Sondheim fan thanks to the boy.

Once Maximillian left the apartment for the afternoon, Marcus turned to the stereo, rotated the CD player to a new album, and let the CD slip to the one song that had been company for so many other times.

Marcus slipped out of his shirt and started dancing around the apartment, singing along with the stereo. His hand on his hips....flying around the room......and occasionally throwing his hands in the air. The music filled the air as she continued to sing about mental illness and Marcus continued to wave his shirt in the air as he sang along with the words.

Marcus flew through the song, and as the trumpets blared and the last note was blared.....the CD went silent. Then there was a succinct clapping in the air. Marcus turned around to see Maximillian standing the doorway. There was a glint of joy and amusement in his eyes.

"Oh God. how long have you been there SIR?"

"From about the point, of developing a cough...." The tall man answered.

"Chronic Organic Syndromes?"

"Something like that yes ... boy..."

Marcus smiled.

"Well at least I got the notes right?" Marcus said with a chuckle.

"That you did young man, that you did..."

Marcus found himself unable to move towards his Daddy. He was embarrassed.

"Sorry that wasn't very butch,...." Marcus apologized.

His Daddy then quickly knelt in front of him.

"What could you possibly...apologize for. I don't want a total butch boy who doesn't be himself, just to fit into a mold of some magazine or bar...I want you, for you.....its actually appropriate for our evening for you to be you....Patricia won't want to meet the piss drinking cocksucker tonight, she'll want to meet Marcus...the young man I am falling for..."

Marcus felt warm inside. Sometimes all it took is this man's touch on his chin to make the worst day or moment just melt away. The feeling of attraction was mutual. He had no idea where this was going....and he did realize since his Mother lived in Oregon, and his sister really didn't have that much of an interest in meeting the men Marcus "slept with" that meeting the parents or relatives was something that Maximillian would have to provide.

"You understand me Pup?" the man asked.

"Completely SIR...."

Maximillian smiled gently at him.

"I forgot my gloves...." He said as he kissed Marcus's forehead.

He reached to the side table and the pair of skintight black gloves. The same gloves that had controlled his very breathe hours earlier. They were the same gloves that Daddy always wore when he smoked a cigar, or drove. Marcus liked the gloves a lot.

Another kiss on the cheek and a simple "See you in 6 hours standing outside dressed for a night out, nice shirt. Surprise me and you'll make me very proud."

"Yes SIR."

Marcus looked up when saying that....connecting with his daddy's dark grey eyes. Oh yes, attraction was fully in place.

"And you should check your bed...there is a package there for you..." Maximillian said as he swatted the top of his head with the gloves.

Maximillian stood and showed the obvious hard cock in his jeans...then quickly retreated to the front door.

"See you then SIR..."

"Good Boy."

Maximillian walked out of the apartment with a great deal of satisfaction. He loved when the boy showed just how limber and flexible he was. There was such a love of music inside this human. It was something he tried to encourage. There were new avenues for both of the men. The boy had started spending Monday nights singing with what he called "Gay Men's Chorus". At first, Max had spent many hours feeling jealous fearing that Marcus would find someone else to serve at these "rehearsals". However, being an immortal with certain abilities allowed Maximillian access to places to see Marcus even though no one saw him.

He stood in the back of the room, and just reached in the energy of the room and removed himself from it. As the lesbian director of the group walked to the front and the men all stood up, Maximillian faded from everyone's view. He stepped quietly to the back of the auditorium and listened. Arpeggios of male voices rose in the air and they brushed over him with a great rush. There were emotions he tasted for the first time in many years. There is a succinct sweetness to the emotion of music creation.

He had not been prepared for the memories that it created. Feeling emotions that had for so long been hidden from view, always let Maximillian return to other eras and interactions in his life. For music there had been one man in particular that affected him the way the chorus was beginning to affect him. That man with Thamos. Every hour preparing a powdered wig had been worth feeling the emotion that the blind man could create. The thing about the blind....they can tell when someone else is there when a logical seeing man...cannot. Maestro knew he was there.

"You stand in the darkness soaking in my sounds...I figured monsignor it was time we introduced ourselves. Although you seem to enjoy your cloak of darkness and mystery. If it was not for your slightly audible purr when I play, I would have not noticed you.." the blind man had said.

"I am Maximillian...."

"You are one of the others....I know that...my gift is yours to enjoy Monsieur Maximillian."

"Play Maestro....feed both of us."

The music would pour out of the musician and into the keys of the instrument. It would be the passion that linger in the room and pound Max with almost arousing force. Therefore, when he sat in the back of the room, and the music of the 200 plus men poured toward him, he almost braced for the impact. The taste of music was quite intoxicating to a point. When he opened his eyes as the arpeggios gained speed, he would see Marcus standing in the tenor section, and an unbreakable joy flowed through him.

It had been just as many years for the brethren to also taste another old friend, the taste of his own pride in someone he cared for. It was a gift that he had only returned once a month to take in. Receiving the emotion and passion of the singers weekly would become almost too much for him to control. Releasing his passion in return was something he couldn't allow. Unveiling his passion while face fucking Marcus, or in a sex club or a movie, theater was different. There would be an explanation of the sudden flood of arousal and intoxication the male humans would feel, not to mention what a wave of energy might do to the females present.

The female director supplied touches of emotion that the brethren had never felt before. Patricia would probably appreciate a good taste of the emotions that flowed into him. While she found Clive her proper mate, feeling the female emotion was something Patricia missed occasionally. Still being a good collector of said emotions, Maximillian found himself sometimes feeding enough from women in shops, or movies to provide Patricia with a taste of those lives.

Patricia had been grateful for many things in Maximillian's life, and was the one who suggested that she finally meet his human. She found his nickname of Pup amusing, as there some things of the homosexual inclination she just didn't understand. Calling a grown man "puppy or Pup" was one of them. Patricia wanted to meet this potentional partner, so she had bought tickets to a popular traveling show. Maximillian had never seen it. She was confident he would enjoy it, and knew that the new companion would easily enjoy it from what she had learned of him.

Clive had been interested as well. Humans that are made companions have a fellow human to help them through the transformative state and the new world it opened a custom to them. Clive was more than willing to assist in that capacity.

Maximillian stepped into his car, and turned the stereo on. The music filled the compartment with Maestro's fifth Symphony. By far, in Maximillian's opinion, the best thing the blind old coot wrote. There was passion even in the recording, and as he turned down Market Street towards home, he wondered if the blind man would appreciate Marcus. He turned up the music as the soft voice in his said "Of course he would..."

The leather man drove into the hills of San Francisco, knowing that this evening his Aunt would meet his future companion, and Marcus would learn more about him that ever before. For tonight, Marcus would be introduced to the truth. His loving boy would learn that the passion that they felt was only starting to build. For also after the play, Maximillian was going to fuck his boy. Something they had only talked about, and the hunt would be over. ...but the bonding and adventure would have only just begun.

Part Eight

Marcus stood at the corner with millions of thoughts flowing through his head. Maximillian had been opening up to him, and letting him learn more and more bout where life had led him before they met on that subway 6 months ago. The boy was also recognizing he had fallen in love with this older man. This man who was capable to make him shiver, by just stepping up to him. Not to mention, the sexual interaction. Maximillian had a limit to this point in their interaction. While Marcus had fed on copious quantities of his Dad's piss, semen was another issue. It was not that he had not worked hard to get that load of white cum down his throat. The Daddy cock had learned to slide down his throat and find great joy in being serviced. They had fucked...but they always used a condom. They had both been tested negative for HIV so Marcus wanted the whole package. Maximillian had resisted.

"I want to taste your seed, Daddy, I want to seal our bonds, and commit myself to you..." was just one of many ways Marcus had put it.

But no matter how the young man described his need, his sexual partner said that his waiting would be rewarded with something much more than just unprotected sex. The bond that Maximillian wanted to offer him would be unlike all others. That would be completely revealed after a night of theater, and a dinner with friends. He looked at his situation and figured waiting to finally bond with a man he wanted to spend the rest of his life was worth it. What were a few more hours, for the rest of his life?

.... rest of his life. Dear God, how those words suddenly had new meaning. Maximillian stood in front of the full-length mirror. He slowly adjusted the knot in his dark purple tie, and quietly reviewed the way he was dressed. The tie complemented the dark brown shirt, and the matching jacket. The tie provided the splash of color that Marcus always appreciated. He wanted to make this evening magical. One doesn't know how one will truly react to finding out the person that they are giving themselves to, is going to give much more than a normal mortal could. The mere act of releasing his seed inside the human pup was the last link in a long chain. First the truth would be revealed to him. There was that chance that Marcus wouldn't understand...what Maximillian was, and rebel against the idea of someone living 1000 years. Not to mention someone living 10 years of human life, over a 100-year period. The life changing that would occur. The magic that would fill the boy, and blossom within his Daddy.

It would begin with Clive picking up the boy and bringing him to Daddies house. Patricia stood behind her nephew with a gentle grin on her face.

"Do you have any idea of how proud I am of you?"

Maximillian breathed heavy.

"Proud, why?"

"We don't all make it to this point of life.... Immortality doesn't mean immune to death...you have survived well..."

Maximillian suddenly found himself enveloped in memories. Memories that haunted of parents dying, of lovers being buried into the sand of Africa, and music reinvigorating a lust within, and a musician saying no. The music of a passion long dead playing on classical music stations, and bringing his fair face to his minds eye.... and providing warmth in the darkness of night.

"He always did love slow gentle melodies...." Maximillian said with a smile.

Maestro appeared in the mirror, and slowly bowed to the man standing in the bedroom.

"He was a love," Patricia said.

"But. He died...."

Maestro faded away in the mirror. A tall figure and a pristine woman stood before him. They smiled and bowed in the similar fashion.

"Mother was a gem, wasn't she Auntie?"

"There is no one ever like her again.... Your father a great servant to her...."

The two figured in the mirror faded.

"But, they died..."

Patricia stepped to the side of her nephew and sighed. She placed her pale hand upon his shoulder.

"Everything eventually dies....even me my boy..."

"Don't say that..."

"You and Marcus, if he accepts the truth, will live far past Clive and I. I have transitioned and the aging will begin. You know that.."

"He might say no..."

Patricia kissed his cheek.

"Marcus loves you....it is in every step. This boy, this servant, is your key to the new change in your life..."

Marcus appeared in the mirror, standing on the side of the road.

Maximillian gasped.

"Dear God, he is so handsome...."

Marcus stood on the street corner in a dark black suit, with a dark green vest covering a starched white shirt. There were boots under the slacks. This handsome man never wore anything else.

"Clive is to arrive soon, and he will come to you..."

"The truth could hurt him...."

Patricia smiled as their reflection returned to the mirror.

"He is your greatest gift...."

...."He is my greatest gift" the boy sighed.

That was when he saw the familiar grey BMW of Clive and Patricia. It glided through the crisp night, brushing the impending fog away as it moved closer.

"What ever the reason for waiting.....I know Daddy loves me, we can get through anything…"

The car came to a stop, and Marcus moved forward.

Clive was in the car alone.

"Good evening, handsome….Mistress and Maximillian await us at his flat…"

Marcus grinned widely.

"They love pomp and circumstance don't they…"

Clive smiled with a knowing grin.

"More than you know…" he whispered.

Marcus didn't hear what he said, but gained the playfulness in his tone. He wrote off the words as something good. The two servants drove up the hill and found themselves coming down to Market Street. They turned left and headed up the hills towards Maximillian's hill house. They talked about the musical they were going to see.

The car pulled up to the home of his Daddy….and Clive stopped on the side. The side entrance was lit softly..

"This is your entrance…..Maximillian is waiting for you…"

"The side entrance…thought that was a fake door…."

"This entrance is more real than you could ever..know"

That time….Marcus understood what Clive said.

"What do you know? That I don't old man…." Marcus said with a laugh.

"Step inside and see….and give to him, like you desire to…and he will give double back..."

"Like Patricia gives to you..."

"She is my life........"

"She is my life........." the slave said.

Patricia stood at the mirror and saw her partner saying the gracious things. She felt the same way.....and she would make sure....to thank Clive properly later. He probably felt the presence of her, and was acting on his best behavior. But, it was those moments of desperate service and devotion that she most appreciated her servant. Clive was more submissive than her nephew's servant, but the love was there. Her being her mistress wouldn't occur without love. ...And that finally was what her darling Maximillian had found...love.

She watched as the young handsome man stepped to the door. He reached for the door handle, and the mirror returned to her reflection. The mirror knew privacy was needed now. She listened as Maximillian stepped down the stairway towards the servant, and lower house. The part of the house where Maximillian's history was, was now where the servant stood.

Marcus let out a simple gasp as the door closed behind him. The walls of the room were of a dark stone. There was none of the thin lines and bright colors of his Daddy's hill house. This was a new part ...that he had never seen before.

He walked into the foyer and stopped dead in his tracks. He had never felt the way he felt now. Marcus found himself looking upon an oil painting of a very handsome man. Dark black fur over his muscular chest, a long dark black beard trailing into the chest hair, and long flowing black hair. Leather pants with large buttons down the crotch, and dark shiny boots. The print was striking.... it was beyond erotic. It was that moment, when he found himself finding the portrait attractive.... was the same moment that he found himself looking into his Daddy's eyes. The green stare was unmistakable.

"Wow...." Marcus said.

He then heard steps coming towards him across the stone floor.

"You like what you see?" the voice asked.

Marcus immediately hardened. There was only one owner of the voice. He couldn't see his Daddy, but knew that low bass voice. Marcus continued to look over the print, and noticed Daddy was leaning against a grand piano, and there was someone playing the keys. All you could see was his hands...as the remainder of the painting had been ripped away.

"I used to love long hair...now I can't wait to cut it off..." the bass voice said.

"Is it really you?...." Marcus asked.

"You know it is boy.... you saw my eyes...the Maestro liked my eyes as well. You have that in common..."

Marcus grinned wide.... but then noticed the signature in the bottom corner.

"SFH, December 21st, 1645."

"I don't understand...." Marcus said.

The tall figure of a man he had come to love suddenly appeared out of the darkness to his side. The man looked up to the painting and smiled.

"Yes you do...."

Marcus turned to his Daddy and saw the tears in his eyes.

"How could that be you...?"

Maximillian took a long breath, and pulled Marcus towards him. He thrust himself forward and kissed the boy. When their tongues touched...he released.

Patricia lay in the large couch with Clive in her arms. They both shuddered.

Marcus found himself in darkness, and light. It looked like he was falling through a lava lamp. Bright shades of red, followed by crimson and then dark red. He then looked back up at the painting.... and it was now complete.

Maestro was breathtaking. He was beyond handsome. The piano came to life.

"Are you sure this is what you want for your birthday Maestro...?" the painter asked.

Marcus found himself shaken by the question. He turned back and saw his Daddy both standing next to him, and leaning against the piano. The pianist replied once again.

"While I am not able to see him, I want to be in this oil with him.... he needs to have something to remember...."

There was a gentle tear in Maximillian's eyes as he leaned against the piano.

The dark red light flowed over him again.

Maximillian stood before the oil painting. He was dressed in black. He had a simple black band around his arm. Patricia walked up to him. Marcus gasped. This was a much younger Patricia.

"The Maestro was your love.... don't destroy his gift" she said. Maximillian ripped at the painting.... the gentle face of the pianist fell to the floor.

Patricia picked up.... the fragment and cried with her nephew.

"I cannot live without him...."

"You must...."

"I will never find another...."

Patricia.... turned to Marcus as if seeing him.

"You will...."

The Maximillian in the display walked into the darkness. Patricia stood before the painting. She turned to Marcus and before his eyes began to age. The grey highlights that he was so familiar with slowly emerged.

"You have..."

The image was flooded with many images. Marcus began to tear as he realized what the images were. They were the lonely life that his Daddy had led. All the emotion, all the dread, all the depression…. flooding through him. Watching as two hundred years flowed by. The boy then knew…what it all meant.

He had not found a normal Daddy. He found something much more.

The red light parted, and Marcus found himself in front of the ripped painting. Maximillian stood before him with tears running down his face.

"I am not a handsome man. I am not a perfect man. But I want to learn what old means with you…"

"How long have you lived?"

"Just short of 900 years…"

Marcus gasped.

"Show me more…."

Maximillian took his boy's hand and led him to the inner part of the house. Marcus's eyes widened as the main room was revealed. There were other paintings. There chairs, and cloths from many time periods. Above the fireplace, was one last painting. A Tall figure with brilliant blonde hair and thick beard, and a fair woman with dark black hair, and a baby in her arms. Within her face, were Maximillian's eyes. Those eyes of green.

"Your parents…"

"Yes…"

"but that means…"

"They died in the late 1300s"

Marcus then turned to Maximillian.

"How?"

"We are called Brethren. We as part of nature, as the fly that has a single day life span.... we just tend to live just a little longer."

"Where do I fit in this?"

"When a brethren reaches his or her 900th year, they mate with a human...that will live out their last 100 years with them. Then the couple grows old together...and dies together."

Marcus gasped again.

"That means.....Clive...."

Maximillian smiled gently.

"Has been in his late 50s for just over 100 years...Patricia met him in Britain after the Civil War was nearing completion in the United States."

Marcus fell backwards...and into Maximillian's arms. He went to move away, but quickly corrected his movement. He stayed in his Daddy's arms.

"That is why you have never fed me?"

"Yes my boy.... to feed you, would make you mine. Period. End of subject."

"But that is what I have wanted."

"Ah, but to live 160 years, instead 60 more.... you probably didn't have that in mind when you had those thoughts. If we bind. It will be for the rest of our lives, through bad and good times. We will always be bound. Unable to survive with each other to counter balance."

Marcus felt the warmth coming from Maximillian, in his words and his body.

"But you had to know the truth first."

Marcus laughed.

"Well this is truth isn't it..."

Maximillian hugged the human tight.

"Yes it is..."

Marcus tore out of his arms and ran back to the foyer.

He ran his hands along the ripped parchment.

"He loved you very much...didn't he..," Marcus asked.

"More than any man has.... till now...my pup," the voice said from the other room.

"And you said, he said no..."

Maximillian walked up to Marcus with tears in his eyes....

He again touched the pup and the walls around them melted away to a dark grey room. Rain was falling outside the windows.

"I cannot be your beloved..." Maestro said.

"I do not understand why..?"

"I am blind.... a cripple.... I am not worthy of such love as you offer."

"You are perfect in my eyes...."

"Eyes that can see through imperfection...."

"I love you..."

"I need you to leave me now...I have music to finish."

The pianist turned to the piano and let the music fill the hall. Maximillian ran from the piano and out the door. The Maestro continued to play his music, and seemed to turn to Marcus.

"And he has. Found a perfect mate.... in you..."

Marcus gasped as the walls returned and the painted froze the past back in place.

"He has..." this time it was a familiar female voice.

Patricia and Clive stood in the main room. In her hands, she held a felt covered frame. It had been meticulously frame to follow the fracture of the fabric. In her hands, she held the missing piece of the portrait.

"You make Maximillian complete..." Patricia said.

"And Maximillian can make you more his servant, than any human will ever be capable...you have felt his power before.."

Marcus could only nod in agreement. He had felt the sensations.

Maximillian turned to Marcus....and smiled through his tears.

"But you have to want my gift freely."

Maximillian dropped to his knees in front of Marcus.

"I want to bond with you unlike any other.....even the Maestro. He was right. I would find someone again..."

Marcus looked down at Maximillian. He saw the love in his eyes. He saw the hunger and felt the need to feed rising inside of him. He lunged forward and kissed his Daddy. They kissed for what seemed like an hour.

"I want to be your boy...your...servant."

A warmth started to grow from the floor around his body. Neither Marcus nor Maximillian noticed the frame left on the rug in the main room, or Patricia and Clive walking up the stairs to the main house. Marcus looked into the deep green eyes and said it again.

"I want to be your boy, your servant. Your guide..."

The warmth grew in temperature until it seemed to consume the human man. Maximillian stood up from his crouch, and as he stood the clothes he was wearing seemed to melt away. He grabbed the back of his lover's head and kissed him deeply.

Marcus felt his clothes dissipate to the touch of his Master's skin. One more burst of warmth, and Marcus felt his Daddy's flesh inside him. The large pierced cock burying itself inside him...one more time.

"Tell me what you want boy.."

"I want to be yours…"

The warmth consumed him.

Conclusion

San Francisco will always be the place the gay men will go to realize their sexual dreams. Straight couples went to Niagara Falls, and male gay couples came to San Francisco and the surrounding area. As you walked along Castro Street there was just a different energy than before, something foreign and unidentifiable if one wasn't homosexual. There was a sense that here anything was possible. It was the last Sunday in September and for a certain segment of the population it felt like Independence Day. The cafés down the sides of Castro Street were filled with men and women dressed in tight leather clothes, and even tighter jeans. It was if the fog had brought in with it a tide of masculinity and roughness, and when the sun burned the fog away everything else remained.

Folsom Street was where the spectacle began actually. Far away from the everyday homosexuality of Castro Street were rows and rows of tents sprouting up. They were to be filled with vendors. Some would be selling trinkets of the latest trend, or t-shirts with humorous sayings, and some would be selling S/M toys and gadgets that people would try out on willing submissives, aching for a new sensation from their dominant. Marcus's favorite part of the vent was the fog slowly burning off, warming up the streets of the fair, and drying away the wet reminiscence of the rain.

The loft they had purchased was two floors up from street and the growing flood of people below. The patio opened to French doors that let in the smell of leather, and sweat. The aroma would only increase as the day proceeded. There would have been times in his life that certain scents hadn't been more arousing than others. That was before he had met his partner, his lover, his Daddy, his Owner; Maximillian.

Marcus stepped to the edge of the doors and looked down at the tents slowly filling up with vendors. A leather gloved hand reached around his waist and a gentle wet kiss of saliva and smoke caressed his neck.

"The fair wont be going for another good two hours...I believe I have plenty of time finish this cigar with you, in the chamber...and we'll need a good shower before heading downstairs anyhow. Why not..."

Another kiss of smoke and saliva, this time dripping down Marcus's neck in a seductive call.

"...Give ourselves a good reason to shower, instead of just removing the sweat of a night..." the voice beckoned.

He then felt the one thing that always made Marcus submit to his Daddy. It was the tug of a sharp tooth against his ear lobe.

"That is not fair Daddy....not fair at all," Marcus whispered as he fell back into his partner's arms.

"I never claimed to playing fair my boy," the voice whispered through another release of smoke.

Marcus then felt the hardness of his partners cock pressing against his furry ass. Smoke began to fill the room in subtle patterns.

"Then, you agree...a cigar and my seed shouldn't be kept.... at bay?" the voice asked.

Marcus sighed as he rubbed backwards roughly against his partner providing a silent answer. A second gloved hand came from behind him and caressed his mouth. It slowly began to make breathing harder as it clamped down over his mouth. The other hand was busily working his left nipple.

"Oh yes.... the boy knows makes Daddy happy...," the voice whispered.

The brief release of the glove was met with a large release of smoke into his face from the side. Marcus sucked in as much smoke as he could. He was familiar with the pleasure that his partner took with smoke and fucking. With the loss of air, the sweetness of the forced smoke now burning his lungs were soon joined with the hardness entering him. Once connected Marcus's chest, the strong hands of his Daddy pulled him quickly away from the window and into the bed. The two men swung around and Marcus braced himself to fall to the bed.

"That's it.... take it all..."

The balls of the large man's crotch slamming into Marcus's ass, and the firmness deep inside him, were always an exhilarating experience. It had been several months since that cock had truly changed him. The warmth pouring inside him and making every bone in his body tremble with an ecstasy that he had never achieved before… and will now only achieve with his Master… was immeasurable. The slight sting of ash falling onto his back and the continuing levels of cigar smoke caressing the scene drew Marcus deeper into submission.

"You want it all don't you boy…?"

The fucking halted. The firm shaft staying deep inside him.

Throbbing but not moving. He had to answer. Marcus could only gasp.

"Answer me…boy."

One firm pounding thrust.

"Yes. SIR I do…"

With one firm grasp of Maximillian's gloves Marcus fell to his back, the hard cock still deep inside him. He then looked up to the older gentlemen that had firm control of him. Maximillian had a devilish grin on his face.

The boy had never failed him once the true sexual interaction had begun. Transforming the boy into a consort had been one of the true joys of Max's life. Seeing the warmth stretch from Marcus's willing eager ass and spreading over his body, and watching the human's eyes widen as the true emotion and essence of sexual contact with Brethren took hold. And when the seed of his loins poured into his consort giving him new senses and new hunger…Maximillian knew this was a mate he would treasure. The waiting had been all worth the conclusion.

"I want it all Daddy…. your ash, your piss and your seed…. all of it inside me…"

Maximillian drew on his cigar and took great amounts of smoke into his lungs. The boy was going to get what he asked so politely for. The hunger would be fed. Maximillian lunged forward throwing the boy's legs into the air. The smoke needed to be released. The animalistic kiss and the moans of pleasure as the cigar's load was released into his partner's mouth, was all Maximillian needed to hear. The seed released inside the boy and the warmth fled outward. Like a blanket of sensuality it covered the block in its silent but arousing effect. Orgasms were much more intense now. For not only was the Master taking his slave, but the slaveboy was truly learning how to respond to the sexual tension and drawing just as much energy out of himself to match his partner's need to fuck.

Marcus was a good learner. The boy also knew not to move yet. The bonding wasn't complete yet. The cigar continued to provide blankets of smoke for the couple as the other deposit was readied. It was not done till the warmth of a morning's worth of piss began to deposit itself deep inside the boy, did Maximillian really take a full breath. He lifted the boy off the bed and in embrace walked towards the shower. They both needed one now.

The shower had been one thing that the boy had helped plan in their new home. Maximillian took great pleasure in building it with him. With four large rainforest showerheads coming out of the ceiling water cascaded down out of the ceiling with thunderstorm strength.

Maximillian went to step in.

"The water isn't warm yet SIR..."

Maximillian smiled.

"I know."

The boy tried to struggle out of his grasp as the Master dragged them both into the cold downpour of water. There were curses. There was laughter. There was the warm of the piss flowing down over both of them, as the water met its warmth. There was caress. There was steam. There was a now soaked three quarters smoked cigar lying at their feet. The warm of the water led to Maximillian lifting his boy onto the shelf and taking the consort's flesh into his hand.

"Ah, not done yet..."

Patricia stood before the mirror and smiled. She was quite enjoying the pleasure her nephew was having. The newness of their connection was still a joy to them both. Charles stepped to her back and caressed his Mistress's shoulder as he tightened her bodice.

"Folsom Street is an hour's drive for us Mistress...." Charles said softly.

"Always the thoughtful one..." Patricia answered.

The Mistress waived her hand and their reflection returned to the mirror.

"They seem happy...."

"Oh they are. They will have their arguments, like we did."

"Yes Mistress"

"Prepare the car...Charles..."

"Yes Mistress..."

Her consort left the room as she finished putting the braids in her hair. No one at the festival would imagine she was 980 years old. There was fear her in body. She could feel it. She had never felt fear before.

She fell to one knee.

No one would guess she was 980 years old. No one when the ambulance arrived would realize that she was alive when the Mayans and Aztecs ruled America. No one in the emergency room would see a woman who had survived the Civil War. No one when the doctor called a heart attack.... would realize there was a women of long life loosing the battle...and carrying on to another place.

No one but Maximillian...who fell to the bottom of the shower in fear. Feeling his Aunt's fear coming to life. Ironic life coming alive to take that which so many might take for granted, and with a single breath Patricia Collins was gone. Another Brethren lost.

"We gather here today to mourn the loss of Patricia Collins," the voice said with a reverent tone. There was a main funeral contingent. There were over a hundred people surrounding the grave covered in roses. Maximillian with a single rose stood with Patricia's Consort of 125 years at his left, and Marcus standing at his right.

There had been times that he never thought this day would come. After several hundred years, what is another hundred years.... just another lifetime to take part in. Patricia had been there through a lot of his. The three men released their roses as the casket was slowly lowered into the ground. Others came to their side, and left their roses with the others.

Many came by them, as Maximillian explained that Charles was selling the house and moving to the compound south of Harrison. Charles had gratefully accepted the offer.

Later in the hallway of the chamber that was long built below the street a large silk painting of four figures was framed. Patricia stood proudly in her dark red velvet dress, with Charles knelt in front of her. Maximillian stood beside his Aunt with his consort on his knees before him, one gloved hand on his shoulder.

"There will come a time when we will just be a painting…"

Maximillian said as he sipped the wine.

Charles sighed.

Marcus then turned to his Daddy with a gentle smile.

"Our adventures have only just begun my MASTER…"

Maximillian looked down into the boy's eyes and saw the yearning and love within them. Maybe the boy was right. There would be time to grieve and then there would be time for new adventures to begin.

"Good Boy…Light my cigar then, will you…?"

He had been to many Folsom Street fairs. There had been the 70s when Folsom Street was a religious gathering. The 80s and 90s there was fun in the sun, until the baby boomers, baby carriages and straight folks with their families joined in. The early 2000's had provided a return to a more private affair. For the owner of the main leather bar on Castro it was the beginning of a new era. Everyone just seemed more sexual and interactive in the past several years. Like an infection wafting over the crowd in the bar the air was filled with tension and release. Since 2017, they had allowed smoking to return to the bars, and cigar daddies returned to his counter.

There was nothing like it.

The old bartender sat in his corner as the new generation of bartender tended to the leathermen's needs. He just got to count the money at the end of the night and maybe even take a young willing soul back to his apartment for some spit swapping and cock worship. But the bootblack stand was never the same as he remembered it. It had been 30 long years since the strapping lad had worked his magic at the stand. He could still vividly remember the cigar daddy that came to his bar, and charmed the love out of the bootblack. The many dances they did in front of the men. A Master and his boy....presenting hours of foreplay for the younger generation to witness. Those days were gone.

The Master was probably long dead and the boy a grieving widow. While Old Guard had slowly returned to the leather community, and ritual replaced created stature, there weren't men like that cigar daddy anymore.

It was that moment that the scent of the cigar hit his nostrils. He turned to follow its trail, to see a Master guiding his boy out of the bar, by the back of his neck. A thick gloved hand along a dark brown neatly trimmed head. Memories were playing tricks in the smoke filled air.

The boy then stopped, turned to his partner, and helped relight the cigar in the Master's mouth. For a second the old bartender caught a glimpse of his face. It was Marcus...as if 35 years had not aged him a day.

The old man tried to stand. The crowd bunched in around him as the leather couple made their way to the door. The couple turned around and smiled at the bartender. The Master tipped his cap in a salute and the boy just smiled.

The bartender blinked his eyes, and by the time he adjusted his eyes through the smoke the couple was gone. Back into the smoke...becoming a memory not long forgotten.

An adventure ...just beginning.

About The Author

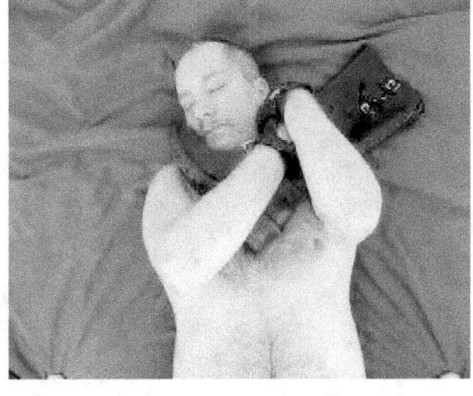

Drew McDiarmid lives in Houston, Texas, where he is a proud member of Bayou City Performing Arts, with both the Gay Men's Chorus of Houston and their small ensemble, VOCALEASE. Drew is 38 years old.

Drew has always had a passion for smoke, and S/M activities that can follow them. Drew spent most of the 90s involved with Orange Coast Leather Assembly in Santa Ana, CA. He also competed in the International Mr. Bootblack Contest at IML in 1997 and 1998, coming in third in 1997. He also volunteered time with Leather Archives and Museum, and served as the Rocky Mountain Regional Coordinator.

Drew would like to thank specific members of the leather community that have helped shape him into the smoke/boot/bondage boy that he is today: Joseph W. Bean, Brian Dawson and his partner Jeff Burnham, SLAVEMASTER, Ned Sheats, Matthew Maistre, Dennis Hatch, Master Trooper Frank Sardone, Bryan Freedman, and Matt Prather.

Without YOU, I am nothing.

www.ingramcontent.com/pod-product-compliance
Lightning Source LLC
Chambersburg PA
CBHW071226260626
47162CB00004B/1437